A Fragile Wife

A Novel

Cynthia Dane
BARACHOU PRESS

A Fragile Wife

Copyright: Cynthia Dane
Published: 14th December 2015
Publisher: Barachou Press

This is a work of fiction. Any and all similarities to any characters, settings, or situations are purely coincidental.

Chapter 1

"I've Been Waiting For You, Husband."

Lana Andrews, real estate queen and all-around rich, domineering bitch, was once again on the floor of her office with a bottle of whisky threatening to spill beside her.

It was a good thing she had a mural on her ceiling. Nothing fancy. Some flowers with intricate vines weaving in and out, creating a cacophony of demurred colors that caught her eye whenever she lie on this floor, half-drunk and on the verge of making the same grievous mistake she always almost made.

I'm going to divorce that asshole.

She thought it once a week at this point. Sometimes multiple times a week. Lana took a swig of her drink and tried not to breathe into the carpet. Difficult to do when her body kept trying to roll against it.

Cynthia Dane

"Chloe!" she called, drawing her foot out of its stiletto heel and letting her toes curl against the warm carpet. "Chlooeee!'

The maid, a young woman with big eyes and thin hair, appeared in the office doorway with shock on her face. "Yes, ma'am?" she asked tentatively. Chloe approached Lana's supine body and looked down into a pair of groggy eyes. "Are you all right, ma'am?"

"I need... I need my phone. It's on my desk."

Chloe looked between her mistress and the desk a few feet away. "One second, ma'am."

The maid stepped around Lana's body and gingerly picked up the large smart phone glowing on the desk. Blue lights flashed, signaling that many messages waited. One of them was doubtlessly from Ken Andrews, Lana's husband of nearly ten years. He was at their downtown office that day. Lana was *supposedly* working at home. If being half drunk on the office floor counted as work. *In some countries, it does.*

Her phone dropped into her hand. Chloe stood above Lana, clasping her hands and looking as if she were about to roll her eyes at this weekly spectacle. "Anything else, ma'am?"

"No. Leave me." Before Chloe could disappear out the door, Lana flung a hand into the air and said, "Wait. If my bastard of a husband comes home, tell him I'm having a conference call and can't be bothered."

Chloe said nothing. Soon enough she was gone, the office door closing behind her. *She'll tell him.* She would if she valued her job. And she should. The Andrews paid a good salary with hefty benefits and bonuses.

- 2 -

It meant dealing with her, of course, but there was a snag to every job.

Just like hiring a younger, pretty girl like Chloe probably meant Lana's husband was sleeping with her.

"Lana," said a terse voice on the phone. She had slammed one of the first numbers in her contact list. "What can I do for you this week?"

"Get me a divorce, Horace," she told her lawyer.

"What is it this time? I told you, he only violates that iron-clad prenup if he cheats on you. And given your two's proclivities… that would be very hard to determine."

"Shut up, Horace."

"So I take it you don't have any evidence of him cheating?"

Am I sure he's cheating? Either way, Horace was right. The only way Ken could violate the prenup they signed ten years ago was if he fucked some little nugget behind his wife's back. But Horace was also right in saying that their kinky love life made cheating hard to prove. For years, Lana and Ken had been swinging, group sexing, everything between here and there. They were regulars at the local BDSM club with first-name knowledge of half the people there. Carnal knowledge, too. While they didn't have an *open* marriage in that they could have casual sex or long term relationships with other people, there were those who came into their bedroom and left very… *happy.* No judge would believe that Lana didn't know about Ken's dalliances. All he had to do was tell said judge that she gave him permission. So many people at the club would probably back him up.

Lana groaned into her phone. "I don't know if he's cheating. He'd be a stupid son of a bitch to try it." Especially with *her* pussy still readily available whenever he wanted it. *Since when do men think with their main brains, though?* "There's gotta be something we can do. I'm gonna murder the man at this point."

"I'll pretend I didn't hear that. And at any rate, I'm still not sure why you call me every week asking me to get you a divorce. Stop drinking and get your shit together, Lana."

Boy, he was *lucky* that he was her cousin! And good at his job. If anyone else talked to Lana like that, she would be hacking off their balls and hanging up their entrails from the flagpole in the front yard. "You're a dick, Horace. See you at Easter."

That was her sign off every week. And every week Horace replied, "See you at Easter."

Lana hung up. She didn't need his shit.

She didn't know *what* she needed. She barely understood what was happening to her marriage.

***

They met twelve years ago, at a regional real estate conference. Ken was an established manager of one of the biggest real estate groups in the area, and Lana was an up and coming bigshot who had sold more properties than anyone else in the state that year. It was natural that they meet each other, introduced via a mutual acquaintance who was interested in getting a head-hunter's fee for bringing Lana into Ken's fold. Lana had ambition. Ken had need for a charming agent who could sell high-ticket properties. What neither of them planned on was Lana charming Ken into drinks at the bar that night.

And then her charming him into bed. Or the other way around. Lana could never remember since more than two drinks were involved that night.

Few people could say that a one-night stand turned into a business opportunity. Then a relationship. Then marriage within two years. When they announced their impending nuptials to the media, other real estate moguls quaked in their loafers. Between these two shrewd minds, it was only a matter of time before the Andrews, as they were collectively called, started beheading the competition. *And then we beheaded each other in the bedroom.*

The furor they whipped up in their everyday lives had a tendency to translate to their private life. Lana lived for the high she got from a big sale, and she lived for the celebration of taking Ken between her legs. Whether he climbed on top of her, she rode him, or he pulled on her from behind to impale her on his cock – who gave a shit. Their life meant taking names in public, taking each other's bodies in private.

The kink came quickly. Ken had dabbled in the switch lifestyle, and Lana was more than curious in both calling her husband a slut and having him defile her when they were alone. Everyone in the local kink scene rolled their eyes when they patrolled the streets of their elite world, looking for new playmates and people to fuck with, mentally and physically.

Lana's thirst for exhibitionism led to them performing many times on stage. *I've been screwed in front of a total of a thousand different people by now.* She felt no shame. Usually, the thought aroused her.

So what happened? For several years, Lana lived for the thrills her husband gave her – and for the thrills they picked up from other people. They were a team. Nobody could think of Lana without thinking of Ken, and vice versa. Sure, they had independent friends and hobbies, but when it came to sex – of which there was a lot – they were a monolith.

Now Lana often stood in their mansion in the Hills, wondering what was missing.

She was a woman who was used to moving on quickly when things dried up elsewhere. She went to three different universities, all before getting her Bachelor's. *Don't get me started on how many grad programs I went through.* Before Ken, boyfriends were like tissues. Disposable. Ken was the first man to really make her feel in love and lust, let alone for so long.

So when she got the feeling she was falling out of love, her first inclination was to sever ties and go her way. Screw Ken.

No, but…

Lana had a game she liked to play. She would wait for Ken to come home, prepared to fall out of love with him… or in love all over again. The latter happened more often than the former. The fact she even considered the former, however, made her heart drop in her stomach.

Which was funny, because she never considered herself a *romantic* person.

A Fragile Wife

***

Ken was late that night. Dinner was at seven, as always, but at six-thirty Lana received a call saying her dear husband was trapped in a meeting and only now leaving. It took at least forty-five minutes to drive that far into the Hills, traffic and weather depending.

So Ken did not arrive home until seven-thirty, his layers of clothing shedding from his skin as Chloe did her due diligence helping the master of the mansion get settled in. This included a small glass of bourbon waiting on a tray that would also take away his tie and cufflinks. The last thing Ken wanted to do when he returned home was go all the way up to the master bedroom just to come back down for dinner.

About time he got home. Lana sat at the head of the dining table, where dinner was kept warm but not yet served. The cook began bringing out dishes the moment Ken walked through the door, so by the time he made it to the dining room he had a plate waiting for him. And a pretty young maid following him around, demurely asking if he would like to have his cigarette now or after dinner.

"He'll have it after dinner," Lana said, lifting a glass of wine to her lips. Ken sat next to her, and the scent of his heavy cologne nearly overpowered steak and vegetables. He sighed as Chloe walked away with the tray of cufflinks and tie.

"Lovely to see you too, Wife."

"I've been waiting for you, Husband."

Those sorts of titles were only exchanged when they were feeling incredibly silly or sarcastic. Right now the sarcasm dripped from their fangs like venom.

Ken slipped his hand over Lana's knee before he even picked up a fork. "If you're not letting me have my cigarette right now, then I'll have to soothe my nerves some other way."

Lana stared at him, feeling his fingers press deeply into her flesh. *Wish I could say it was turning me on.* She drank her wine and said, "I don't want to smell it while I'm eating."

"It doesn't smell, Lana. It's vapor."

"It reeks." Ken quit smoking real cigarettes shortly after they married, but was one of the first on board the vape trend. He tried to tell Lana that it was healthier, had no smoke to stain the walls, and, better yet, *didn't smell.* Well, no, it didn't smell like cigarette smoke, but Lana could smell whatever he put in it to give it flavor. Ken could smoke whatever he wanted in his office. At the dinner table? Lana was queen.

Ken cleared his throat. "Sorry I'm so late, Bunny," he mumbled. *Oh, Bunny.* There were few things that people didn't know about them. The fact that Ken called his wife "Bunny" was one of those secrets. Not even Chloe had heard him call her that. "One of the attorneys was late for our afternoon meeting, so we ran over. So far over that I have to go in early tomorrow to finish the blasted thing."

Lana stabbed her food, although gingerly brought it up to her mouth like the lady her mother tried to raise her to be. "That's unfortunate."

"I'm beat."

If Ken cleared his throat one more time, Lana would probably have to strangle him. Instead, she ignored him, knowing damn well what he wanted. One of the things he wanted was to push his hand farther up her thigh, trekking beneath her skirt and playing with the tops of her stockings. *I've never met a man who loves tights and stockings more than this pecker.* All Lana had to do to get laid was show up in nothing more than lingerie. As long as that lingerie had sheer black tights with lace around the trim. She saved the fishnets for the nights she really wanted to dominate him. Tonight was not one of those nights.

"I'm sorry to hear that, Kenny." She hoped he didn't hear the lifelessness in her pet name for him. As she ate, drank, and considered her nerves, Lana put her hand on his knee as well, squeezing it for dear life. "I know you work hard."

They both worked hard. Sometimes Lana stayed home, sometimes Ken stayed home, and sometimes they both went into the city to run meetings and deal business. Exhausting. They put on a front that had helped them castrate the masses for going on a decade now. The power couple. The power *hungry* couple. The formidable pair that no one could defeat unless they were truly that shrewd or had a whole army behind them. Lana and Ken were like peas and carrots. Yin and Yang. Love and lust. They complemented each other, filled in each other's weaknesses, and had reached a point three months into relationship where they were already finishing each other's sentences – and orgasms.

Two such intense personalities seemed doomed for the start. People didn't think they would last more than three years.

They defied everyone by making it five. They won their own bet by coming up on their tenth anniversary.

They were going on a second honeymoon. An island in the Bahamas where, as Ken whispered into her ear when he brought forward the plan, "they could fuck naked on the beach and nobody would care. Except maybe those bastard sharks and jellyfish." Lana wouldn't say no to beach sex, although she had to talk to her gyno about the possibility of her monthly nuisance rearing its ugly head during her second honeymoon. They were into some fairly kinky shit, but Lana drew the line at anything involving blood. At least they had pills for that now.

It reminded her that she also needed to ask about more permanent birth control options. She had been on the pill for years, since before meeting Ken, but by now she was about as interested in having children as she was interested in watching her husband sleep around with someone ten years younger than her. Unless it was Lana's idea, of course. *Why not? Sometimes it's hot seeing some twenty-year-old get a taste of my husband's brand of fucking.* Only if she got to watch, though. And pick out the girl. And seduce her into her husband's lap on his behalf. That was most of the fun.

She looked at him now. She looked at Chloe, walking through the dining room with refills for the wet bar in the corner. The maid glanced at the back of Ken's head before leaving.

If he's not fucking her now, she's going to try it eventually. Ken was handsome and stinking rich. Powerful. Chloe knew he could

Dom, and she seemed like the kind of girl who wanted to sub for the right man. She had nothing to lose – except her job.

"Lana."

She looked back at Ken, tasting the tip of his fork before patting the top of Lana's hand on his lap. "What is it?' she asked.

"I was telling you that I need to get up at five tomorrow. Will it bother you?"

She could be a light sleeper. If he got up before her, it sometimes caused her to wake up and not be able to go back to sleep. This was his polite way of telling her to wear her earplugs.

"I will wear my earplugs." She forced a smile. "The ones you got me for my birthday." What a romantic gift. To be fair, he also bought her a diamond watch and filled the house with fifty dozen red roses. The poor chef, who was apparently allergic to flowers, had to take an emergency trip into town to grocery shop and bring back take-out for Lana's dinner.

Ken lifted her hand from his lap and kissed her fingertips. "You look beautiful tonight."

"Thank you." She reclaimed her hand in the name of using utensils and finishing her wine. "I thought of you while I freshened myself up for dinner. I thought, 'How could I get my husband's dick hard when he steals one glance at me?'"

Ken leaned in, his breath whisking into her ear. "It worked."

"Hmph." Lana pulled away. "Well, while you were working hard today, I…"

"Called your cousin to ask him to help you divorce me?"

Lana put down her utensils with a huff. "Stop it."

"Don't play coy, Lana. I heard you a month ago when you were drunk on the floor. Remember?"

"I said stop it."

Ken shook his head. "I don't know what's gotten into you lately. I think this second honeymoon will be good for us." He picked up the bottle of wine and refilled his wife's glass. "Assuming you don't serve me with divorce papers like Caroline did to Dominic Mathers right around the time we got married."

"A woman after my own heart." Lana admired any woman with the balls to divorce her husband on their twentieth anniversary.

"I'm sure she is." Ken rubbed her arm, his eyes darting between her demeanor and the soft skin beneath his touch. "Are you restless, Bunny? After this shit of a week we'll have a night or two to spare. We could go to the club and take in some of the energy." He watched his wife drink her wine. "Or we could go to the Château and see our kitten."

Neither appealed to her. Not going to the club and putting on her fake smile to tell the world she and Ken were still powering through people like an army. Nor did she salivate at the thought of going higher into the mountains where they kept a mutual mistress in a discreet manor. *She costs us a pretty penny.* They were full-time patrons, although she took on other clients when they weren't around. But in return for their copious amount of money, Lana could call the Château up at any time

A Fragile Wife

and say they were coming for their kitten's pussy whenever she wanted. They could take her out for dates, like to the club where they paraded her around like their slave. Money bought a lot of things. Including women more than willing to play the role of mistress.

That thought was the only thing to make Lana smile all day.

"Perhaps the Château, if we can spare the trip. I suppose I've been itching to pinch that woman's nipples. For you, of course."

"That's my girl."

Lana gave her husband her fake smile. The *real* fake smile. Not the one he knew about, the one she used to beguile others when they had a front to create. This was the smile she used for him. The one he assumed was her real, natural smile. The bastard had no idea – it almost made her feel bad for him.

Cynthia Dane

Chapter 2

"My Wife Should Do Many Things."

Lana pampered herself after her shower that night. She spritzed on her favorite scent, rubbing lotion into her legs, her arms, the back of her neck as she let her strawberry blond hair dry on top of her head. Her favorite white silk robe draped over her limbs and breasts. She wore nothing beneath, preferring to let the fresh air of the master suite stimulate her skin. Sure enough, looking into her mirror revealed both of her nipples poking through the silk. *Still as perky as the day I turned sixteen.* Lana was not the most endowed, and that was on her side. Ken always raved about her nipples more than anything else, anyway.

Sensitive nipples. It didn't take much, like the silk brushing against them.

- 14 -

Lana was alone. Her husband was in his office, finishing up preparations for the next day's early morning meeting. Lana finished off her nightcap and then berated herself for drinking so much that day.

Eventually, she got up and went down the hall.

Ken was at his desk, back toward the office door. Lana quietly latched it behind her. Her husband only kept a meager fire beneath the stone mantle and the soft glow of his desk lamp. Glasses graced his head – Lana could see the black frames behind his ears all the way from where she stood.

She said nothing as she approached her hardworking husband. Lana let her hands announce her arrival, wrapping over both of his shoulders and giving a light massage.

"You need to come to bed if you're getting up so early," she said into the top of his head. From that angle, she could see the specks of steel gray emerging after working so hard for so many years. Ken was only nearing forty, but most of the men in his family grayed earlier than this. Lana looked forward to it – a little. There was something about a man with steel-gray hair making love to her with raw, experienced passion that turned her on. *At least something is turning me on right now.* She blamed hormones. It was better than facing the truth – that perhaps Ken wasn't enough anymore.

Lana sighed as she rubbed her husband's shoulders.

"I'll be there soon. I need to finish this up and then unwind."

"By the time you're done unwinding, it'll be midnight and you won't get enough sleep."

"Oh well."

Lana pressed her thumbs into his shoulder blades. "Hurry up, then."

"Keep touching me like that and I may be able to kill two birds with one stone."

As he pulled folders toward him, perusing images of properties they were buying and selling, Lana continued to massage his shoulders and upper back. In any normal marriage this would be nothing more than a moment of one spouse taking care of the other. Except they weren't normal. They weren't vanilla. Everything they did in their intimate moments was laced in kink.

Lana could easily slip into dominant or submissive, demanding or serving at a moment's whim. In public, she preferred the more domineering persona, including with her husband, but in private, she had no issues giving a well-deserving husband everything he needed to feel better after a long day at work.

It also helped that the longer she touched him, the more Lana awakened to her dormant sexual desires. *We haven't had sex in days.* While not unusual sometimes, it did disconcert her after a while. In the early days of their relationship, they had sex every single day. Sometimes more than once. And "early days" meant as late as two and a half years. Unsurprisingly, it was marriage that eventually slowed them down. Marriage and going into business together. Suddenly they were in their thirties and more tired.

Lana still thought they had a healthy, voracious sex life. She craved his touch and he yearned for her. Other people came and went, but they were each other's constant. Not just business partner, but life partner.

Or so she told herself for years. As of late, as many calls to her cousin and lawyer could attest, she second-guessed everything about her marriage. There was going through the motions, and then there was trying to improve things. She didn't have the energy for either at the moment.

When Ken flipped the folders shut, she let out a sigh of relief. When he pulled a key from his pocket and opened the top drawer to deposit it for safe and confidential keeping, Lana ran her fingers through his thick head of hair and asked him why he didn't put the folders in the second drawer, since this one looked stuffed full of business crap.

"I've got other things for safekeeping in there."

"Oh? What?"

Ken slammed the drawer shut and locked it. "Nothing that would interest you."

What?

Her husband leaned back in his chair, pulling his electronic cigarette from his front pocket. Lana moved away before she inhaled whatever scent he puffed on tonight. *I suppose it's better than cigars.* Maybe that's what he kept hidden in the second drawer. *That's going to drive me crazy now.* She and Ken did not keep secrets. When people asked them how their relationship remained so seemingly strong, that was her answer. "*No secrets.*

We tell each other everything. I know where all of his things are, and he knows mine." Apparently it was bullshit.

Knowing there might be something between them made Lana do certain things. Like try to futilely get into her husband's good graces, even if she was already in them. The mind didn't always know that.

"My husband is so weary." She leaned against his desk, loosening the sash of her robe and opening it enough to show him how naked she was beneath. "He should lie back in his chair to enjoy his cigarette."

Her eyes bore into his. Determined, almost spiteful. Ken was the only man who would not flinch under such a gaze. He held it with his own, pushing back in his chair and taking the first drag of his relaxing smoke. Cherries. It would be cherries.

"And my wife should do many things."

Lana pulled open the top of her robe, exposing her hardened nipples to the warm air of her husband's office. It turned on the part of her brain that told her to serve him.

There were women who lived that life. Every day, their Doms and Masters came home, expecting to be waited on, to be served. The women got off on it. Everyone in the situation got off on it. Lana was not one of those women. When she chose to serve her husband – for he was the only person in the world she would *serve* – it was with nothing but love. Foolhardy love, perhaps, but love nonetheless.

She thought she felt love inside her as she eased down onto her knees and ran the palm of her hand over his stiffening cock. His pants obscured it, but Lana knew which lines to look for. It also helped that her touch hardened him enough to make him groan on his cigarette.

"Tell me what you like," Ken grumbled on his device. "Know your place, but tell me what you like."

"Yes, sir." Lana unzipped him, letting her fingers dance over the soft cotton of his briefs before finding the skin of his cock. She had felt and seen this thing a million times in her life, but now, more than usual, she had to make Ken think it was as good as the first time.

She also had to give herself completely over to the headspace of servitude. She wasn't just Ken's wife. She was his trophy. The hot, sharp woman he plucked from some promising company and made *his*. The first time they had sex, he slammed her into the bed and drove himself into her so hard that tears fell from her eyes. Not tears of pain or fear. Tears of relief that she had finally found a man who could satiate her hunger *more* than the usual.

To many, Ken was an average man by himself. He was handsome, but didn't stand out in a room of other handsome men, especially since he fell on the shorter side and didn't do much with his look. He was sharp, smart, and witty, but kept to himself unless otherwise provoked or if with very close friends. Even his cock was average. Lana certainly had much bigger in her days. The difference? Men with big cocks had a tendency to rely solely on that. They knew they could get away with women being amazed with only that. Men like Ken had *skill*. They knew how to use their cocks to bring a woman to such pleasure that she didn't know where she was or what her name was. Lana would take that over a big cock for the sake of it any day.

Plus, she had a secret. Well, not so much a secret as biology.

She was small from every angle but her stature. Small as in those men with big dicks often struggled to get them in her, whether her pussy, her ass, or her mouth. *Of course, Kenny loves watching that.* They went through a phase three years ago where they rounded up every hot man with a dick over nine inches and gave them a go while Ken watched in great amusement. *He said the faces I made as I struggled to take them were the hottest thing he had ever seen.* She wished she could say she enjoyed it as much as he did.

So even though Ken Andrews didn't boast the biggest dick around, it was big enough for *her,* and that was all that mattered.

I know every inch of it. She gazed at his flesh, at the hair curling around his base and creeping up the sides. His uncut head enticed her lips, but she held back, opting to push her thumbs into his folds and watch the precum emerge. She knew exactly what that would taste like. She had sucked her husband so many times that she could deep-throat him in her sleep.

"I like the way you smell," she whispered, running both hands through his hair and along his shaft. "It's so… animalistic."

"Is it? I don't smell nearly as good as you. I'm sure."

Who knew if that was true? The way Ken acted when he shoved his face in her pussy sure made it seem like she was the headiest woman in the universe. All it took was one second, and Ken was devouring her, tasting whatever he could. For Lana, it was subtler. She liked to build up her arousal with her husband's natural scent. Let it take control. Take over. Take her to a place where the only thing that mattered was their mutual pleasure.

"And I love how hard you get for me." Ken was a man. He got hard for any hot woman – and occasional man – crossing his path. Lana fell into that category, didn't she? Her husband was still attracted to her. He still desired her, even after their numerous rounds in bed and knowing her deepest, darkest parts of her heart. If that wasn't love, then what was?

"Nobody gets me harder, Bunny."

Ken pushed his chair back, the wheels creating a groove in the carpeted mat beneath him. *So that's how it is?* He was going to take full advantage of her behavior right now. Lana knew she had no choice but to kneel between his legs and make him feel like the king of his castle.

They were a "split down the middle" kind of couple. Sex and gender aside, they strived for true equality. They took turns paying. They took turns driving – although Lana didn't care much for driving and would rather take a driver or let her husband have the wheel. They paid equal shares of their stocks and properties. Even this mansion they called home for the past seven years was half and half.

And yet, Ken could become incredibly alpha when Lana even so much as suggested serving him.

He's still a man at the end of the day. He wanted his wife on her knees and sucking him off. He wanted her spreading her legs for him. He *wanted* her begging for his virility. Every so often? Lana wanted to feel that too. Like she was a tool. A possession. A means to her husband's orgasmic end.

She didn't fully enter that space until she sucked on the tip of his cock, her hand stroking his hard, erect shaft as Ken continued to smoke above her.

"Fuck, Bunny." Ken closed his eyes, let his head roll back against his chair, and took languid drags of his cigarette. *That's right. This is your moment, baby.* Her hardworking husband deserved to have his wife giving him pleasure at the end of a hard day. What had Lana done? Get drunk on the floor of her office and imagine her husband tail-chasing their nubile maid. Hardly productive.

She had also called her lawyer – all right, her *cousin* – and demanded he help her get a divorce. Again. The Lana who currently served her alpha husband felt a crimson-colored shamed. How could she want to give up moments like these?

No, it wasn't about giving them up. It was never about being tired or bored with Ken in the bedroom. That was impossible. The man was more adventurous than her. *He's the one who asked me to peg him all those years ago.*

No, all the thoughts of divorce were about something else entirely.

"Eat my cock, baby," Ken muttered on his cigarette. "I wanna feel it all the way down your throat."

Lana braced her hands on his spread legs, running her tongue up and down his shaft as her throat wetted and the rest of her mouth salivated for him. *People say I have such a big mouth.* They said that figuratively. Lana Andrews was infamous in every social circle for speaking her mind and making friends and enemies in the aftermath. In reality, she had a tiny mouth. When she was a kid, she had to have extensive dental work done to make sure there was enough room for all the adult teeth she kept cramming in there. Doctors expressed concern that she would choke on her own tongue one day. While her mouth did grow as she got older, it was still relatively small.

So when her husband told her to swallow his cock, she had to be careful.

Like I'm not going to do it. How could she say no to a command like that? How could she turn away from the very thing offering to make her feel connected to her husband again? *Not like I don't know how to do this.* Deep breath, relax the gag, and slowly slide Ken's cock all the way down her throat.

He was a patient man. He knew how to lie back, have his smoke, and let his wife take care of the rest. She was there to serve him, after all. He needn't do a thing.

Lana lowered her lips to his base, feeling his whole length fill her mouth, her throat. His head threatened her gag, but it almost never won. Not after this long together. Before she met her husband, Lana always had issues giving men head. They were too eager, choking her. Or they were way too big, hurting her jaw and again, choking her. Or, the pettiest thing of all, they complained about the placement of her teeth. As if she would bite them! On accident, anyway.

Ken was one of the first men she could enjoy this side of oral sex with. He didn't fuck her throat without fair warning. And he fit! Bless this man's perfect biology. Truly as if he were made for her enjoyment.

"Look at me, Lana."

She glanced up, throat easing off him before taking his length again. Ken withheld a groan, but she felt him shudder. She also saw his eyes glaze over as he smoked his cigarette and watched her devour him. Her fingers stroked his sack until her index finger and thumb attempted to circle around his base and squeeze.

"I'm glad to see you behaving so well tonight," Ken continued, one hand lowering to pet the top of her head. Wet blond hair fell to the side of Lana's face. "You've been behaving strangely lately. What's all this talk about divorce? Don't you love me anymore?"

She hummed on his cock, making her husband grip both handles on his chair. Of course she still loved him.

"That leads me to wonder if you're tired of having sex with me. Don't I let you know other men? If you're feeling that much desire for someone else, all you have to do is talk to me about it. But I think you like my cock too much for it to be that."

He took another drag of his cigarette. Lana pulled off him, letting her saliva create a bridge from her lips to his cock. Her fingers broke it and rubbed it into his skin. A man could never be too wet. "Don't mind my strange whims, Kenneth," she said. His real name came out when she was submitting to him. "They change with the phases of the moon."

"Oh, I know."

She wrapped her tongue around his tip and savored the delightful taste of his precum. Lana held his cock still as she took all of him into her throat again, her breaths large and unwavering in her chest.

"Do you like doing this, Wife? Do you like having my cock inside you?"

Another hum traveled down his shaft.

"Of course you do. Touch yourself until you're wet enough for me."

Lana made a show of keeping him halfway in her mouth as she flung back the skirt of her robe and rubbed the inside of her thighs. In truth, her pelvis swelled in heat, every inch of her thinking about her husband taking something other than her throat. Sure enough, when her fingers touched her pussy, she found it in the advanced stages of preparing for him.

She pulled apart her nether lips so she could feel herself dribble down her thighs.

"You know..." Ken tossed his smoke onto his desk and folded his hands across his stomach. "I don't appreciate you fucking with my feelings like that. If you don't have a real grievance with me, then don't do that. And if you do? You need to tell me. I don't like having a knife twisted into my gut any more than you do, Lana."

She didn't say anything. She knew her lips' place was on his cock, bringing him the relaxing pleasure he deserved.

"You know I love you, Bunny. It almost makes me sad that I have to punish you."

Her thighs quivered. The more she fell into her headspace of servitude, the more she liked the idea of her husband making an example out of her.

Ken checked his watch. "I still need to rinse off in the shower and get my ass to bed. I'll have to punish you here. Stop touching yourself and get up."

She obeyed, but only because she liked that tone in his voice. Ken knew how to speak to her. Even when he was about to go 180 on her naughty ass, he could keep his tone low and reasonable. Yet Lana could see it in his eye. The look of a Dom who had to take matters into his own hands.

"Let me see your body."

Lana pulled open her robe, the sash dangling toward the floor as her breasts poked out and her blond pubic hairs called coyly to her husband. She may be not much younger than Ken, but she knew how to take care of herself. Years of careful eating – since she had to take into account the calories in alcohol – exercising, yoga, and endless trips to the dermatologist meant she still had smooth skin, perky tits, and only minimal stretch marks and cellulite. Some things could not be helped, after all.

Yet even with her imperfections, she still felt confident, especially in front of her husband. Ken never gave her the impression that he found her anything but 100% fuckable. *My confidence isn't entirely tied into that, but I won't lie and say that it doesn't make me feel good.* Ken's expression didn't change now, but he looked her up and down, admiring a body he had touched and penetrated a hundred-thousand times.

He had fucked her, smacked her in the appropriate places, and come on almost every inch of her skin in the span of a dozen years. And yet he still looked at her as if he were excited to do it all over again.

"Turn around and bend over."

Lana bristled. "Are you going to spank me, Kenneth?"

"Do you want me to spank you?"

She shrugged, indifferent. "Only if you believe I deserve it."

"No. You won't learn anything from a spanking right now." Ken leaned forward, his erection between him and his wife as he caressed her hips. "You need me to punish you with something other than my hand."

Lana glanced at his erection.

"Yes, Bunny. Now do as I say. Turn around and bend over for me."

The carpeted mat was soft against her feet as she turned and braced her hands against her husband's desk. *He better make this good.* Lana wanted to feel properly punished. If Ken knew what was good for him, he would make her feel like the most obedient, grateful submissive in the universe.

I hope so. I need it.

"Spread your legs."

She eased them open, feeling the carpeted mat turn into the natural hardwood of the floor.

Cynthia Dane

"Show me your cunt."

Cunt. Lana loved that word. It was right up there with "bitch" in her favorite things to call herself and the parts of her body. Other women danced around the harsh vulgarities. To a point, she understood. They weren't interested in reclaiming the terrible things men had called them for generations. Lana didn't mind. She would do it. She would look her husband in the eye and tell him to call it her cunt, especially when he intended on taking it for his. God, *hearing* those harsh sounds fall from his lips and growl in his throat made Lana feel the right amount of belittled and controlled.

She pushed her hand between her legs and once again opened herself. This time, however, it was to her husband.

"Is this satisfactory?" she asked with only a hint of sarcasm. Lana couldn't help it. Sarcasm was her natural speed. "Or should I give you more?" She rubbed her clit, moaning, feeling her fingertips grow wetter the more she stimulated herself in front of Ken's eyes.

"I want to hear you beg for it, Lana. Beg for your punishment."

"Please..." She pressed her breasts against the desk, reveling in the coolness against her nipples. "Punish me with your cock, sir. I've been misbehaving."

"What did you do?"

Lana sucked in her breath, gazing at a stack of papers awaiting her husband's signature. "You know what I've done."

"Now, Bunny, I want to hear you say it."

Did she have to? This was probably a conversation best had when they weren't having sex. "I doubted our marriage long enough to call my cousin again."

"What else? I'm sure you've been misbehaving in other areas." Ken teased her wet entrance with the head of his cock. "I want a full confession, Lana."

She snorted. Like hell she was going in that deep – unlike him. "That's it for today. Now fuck me before I…"

"Before you what?"

Lana threatened to back onto him. "Before I do it for you."

She expected him to pin her down and make her behave. Instead, he tapped her ass and said, "Your eagerness precedes you. You know what they call women who can't wait to get punished with a man's cock, right?"

Ah, yes, one of Lana's most favorite games. "Why, I believe they call them sluts, Kenneth."

"The word slut has never suited you, Bunny. Pick a different one."

She gritted her teeth with a smile. "Call me a whore."

"You always go for the most scandalous words, Lana."

Muscles tightened as she craned her head over her shoulder. "That's one of the reasons you love me, baby."

"You definitely make it interesting." Ken grabbed her hips and brought her onto his cock, his length filling her, pushing deep until she was gasping against his desk. Her knuckles were already white from squeezing way too damn hard.

He gave her two easy thrusts. Then he showed her no mercy.

Cynthia Dane

"Shit!" Lana slapped a hand against her husband's desk as his cock attempted to take her by surprise. "Oh, fuck!"

"That's what I like to hear." Ken was the kind of man who was way too composed when he did his wife. When they were like this? It turned Lana on like nothing else. If any man was going to take control of her, it better be a man who only started growling when he fucked like this. Lana didn't have room in her life for men who lost it the moment they started pumping away like famished idiots.

"Fuck me, Kenneth!" Her body was pushed against the desk, her breasts trapped against stained oak and her pussy stretched to its meager limits. "For the love of *God!*"

This was what a few days without sex did to her. Turn her into a screaming banshee.

"That's right, Lana." Ken wasn't louder than her, but she could hear him, and that was all that mattered. "Take my cock."

He grabbed her by the sides, pulling her up far enough to slip his hands beneath her robe and clutch her breasts. *Oh, no, I'm taken.* Her husband behind her, inside her, in front of her... if Lana was going to bottom for any man in the world, it was one who knew how to do this to her... who knew how to tame the wild tigress she saw herself as.

Ken's thrusts increased. Soon she was wet enough for him to take her so hard that she heard nothing but his skin slapping against hers. *Oh my mother fucking fuck fuck!* She balled her hands into fists and pressed them against the desk.

"Punish me, sir!" She lived for this. For the sheer amount of attention she received from him, his cock stretching her open and claiming her innermost chambers. His hands all over her. His breath increasing. "*Fuck* me!"

"That's right, Lana." Ken pushed her onto the table, forcing himself into her as she moaned against the papers in need of signing. *I just signed them with my DNA. How's that?* No doubt more than a little saliva got all over those pristine white pages. "You can't be satisfied, can you? You're always looking for your next thrill to get you by."

She whimpered into his papers, her hips slamming against the edge of the desk from the impact of his thrusts.

"You're a whore, aren't you?"

The power in that word nearly sent her to the edge. *Yes, yes, call me a whore you bastard.* Demean her, dirty her, make her feel like her entire existence circled around taking pleasure into her body. Her husband's pleasure.

"Does it feel good?" Ken gave her an extra hard thrust in case she wasn't feeling good enough. "Do you get off on men fucking you in the cunt?"

Yes, yes, and more yes.

Too bad Lana was past the point of forming coherent words. She was already coming, her pussy searching for more of her husband's cock to take deeper. As the quick orgasm subsided, Ken pulled up her hip and slammed into her. They had entered the phase of it being all about his pleasure now.

"Fuck me! Fuck my cunt! *Fuck!*"

"Good." Ken grabbed a chunk of her hair and pulled her head back. "Beg for it!"

"Yes! Give it to me!"

"Are you a filthy woman who needs to be punished?"

Every word lit a spark within her. The nastier he got, the hotter *she* got. "For fuck's sake *yes!*"

"And what do women like you get as their punishment, Lana?"

The pleasure was getting to her again. She knew Ken was close. His heavy breaths, the intensity of his thrusts, and that sweet tone in his throat told her she was about to get her punishment. It made her relax around his cock – as much as she could, anyway! – and prepare to accept his climax into her body.

"What do they get?"

His shouts startled her in all the right ways. Just as he was about to ask again, Lana cried back, "They get...!" She couldn't say it, but they both knew what she was thinking.

He proved she was right by holding her down on his desk, his cock stilling deep inside her as the first and second bursts of his seed came.

They were hot inside her. Lana screamed into the desk as she felt them, her body nothing more than a receptacle for her husband's needs, wants, desires, *wishes.* He could use her however he wanted. He could throw her on her back after this and fill her up more. He could come on her face for all she cared. Make her swallow it as it hit the back of her throat. Coat her breasts, her stomach...

Her thighs...

Those last ones got the final part of Ken's orgasm as he pulled out in time to cover her left thigh. Between that and fluids flowing out of her with carefully timed contractions of her inner walls, Lana was done.

Punished, and done.

"My gorgeous girl," Ken said, wrapping his hand gently around the front of her throat and easing her onto her side. Liquid spilled down her leg until it wrapped around her knee, threatening to touch her husband's desk. "At least I'll always have a place to shove my dick and let loose what makes me a man."

Lana would've cackled into her arms if she had the strength.

Her husband sank back into his chair, staring at the ceiling as he attempted to catch his breath.

"And to think... I just showered." Lana stood up, covering her ass with her robe before leaning against the desk. She left the front of her robe open and legs slightly spread so Ken had a good view of what he had done to her. "At least I was sufficiently punished. There is that."

Ken regarded her with a stoic visage. "Isn't that what you wanted?"

"I want lots of things."

"I know that. You have the most voracious appetite of any woman I know."

"I could say the same thing about you."

Ken managed a wan smile. "I'd offer to give you another round, Bunny, but I really need to wash up and turn in. I'll do you again tomorrow."

Cynthia Dane

Lana stepped forward, licking her fingers and patting down a tuft of his hair. "You'll fuck me whenever I damn well please, whore." She could throw that right back at him. With a pat to his cheek, Lana moved away, tying her robe close to her body as she mentally called dibs on their master suite. "Good night, Kenneth."

He watched after her with a look she couldn't read. Was he wistful? In love? *Bored?* "Good night, Bunny. Be there soon."

Lana twiddled her fingers at him before opening the door and stepping out into the hall.

An empty cup dropped at her feet.

"Uh..." Chloe stepped back, tray slammed against her breasts. "Excuse me, ma'am... I was going to... give Mr. Andrews..."

"Sure you were." Any good feelings Lana had dissipated the moment she saw this tart standing outside the door. *She was listening to us screw like kinky assholes.* She had to contain a smile. Lana did love a good game of exhibitionism. Too bad she didn't care much for her maid or the constant thoughts she had of Chloe going into Ken's office for the sole purpose of *giving* him something. Like a blowjob, probably. *That's my job, you useless...*

"I'll be going. Good night, ma'am." Chloe scurried away. Too bad. If she stuck around to watch Lana saunter down the hall, she would've had a great view of the sensual mess making its way down to her mistress's ankle. *I need another shower, the bastard.*

A Fragile Wife

Finally, Lana released her cackle, letting it echo in the wide halls of the mansion she paid half for. *This is my half.* The rooms full of debauchery and marriage-crumbling mind games belonged solely to the Queen of Kink.

Chapter 3

"Nice Ass, Mr. Andrews."

No time like the present to get some vitamin D, was something Lana always thought when she had nothing else to do and the day was warm enough for a bikini. So early the next day she dressed in her favorite black two-piece and wandered out back to the pool, where husband Ken did his twenty laps of butterfly strokes.

She had forgotten he was due home already, let alone after lunch. After his early morning meeting, Ken texted her saying he was canceling his afternoon appointments to spend much-needed time at home. Lana had hoped that meant some time for her, but here they were, on opposite ends of the earth even though they were only a few yards away from each other.

"Oh, my studly muffin of a prime-meat man," she said, well aware that he couldn't hear her as she stretched out on a lounge chair. Lana lowered her sunglasses and draped a barely-there sheet over her. "Making all of that noise when all I want to do is relax." She should have brought her music.

Or at least her E-book tablet with the fancy ink that let her read in the sunlight. Not that she knew what she would read. The last time Lana read a novel was at least two years ago. Who had time? If she read, it was shit like *The New Yorker* or *Reader's Digest*. Or articles on the internet. Sometimes she wondered if she had adult ADHD, since her ability to concentrate on the written word was next to nothing. *And yet I come so easily.* Her sister had adult ADHD, and the main thing she always griped about was taking forty-five minutes to come because she kept getting distracted during sex. *If I had that problem, I would die.*

Good thing she didn't have the problem.

With no peace and no distractions, Lana stared at the sky, catching the few clouds that made their way in the big, blue expanse that was the cosmos. *That one looks like a tree.* When she turned her head, she changed her mind and decided it was a mushroom. *That one's a dick.* Never let be said she wasn't focused on only one thing.

The incessant splashing stopped in the pool. Lana glanced over, catching the exact moment her husband heaved himself out of the water and onto the edge of the pool. His black swim trunks clung to his muscular thighs – oh, and his butt too. Lana whistled as he walked by, bending over another lounge chair to pick up a towel.

"Nice ass, Mr. Andrews."

Ken draped the white terrycloth over his head and walked to where his wife lay, sunning herself. Or at least until her husband blocked out the sun. "Nice tits, Mrs. Andrews."

She gestured to her cleavage sticking out of her bikini top. "These oldthings? I need to get my husband to buy me a new pair."

Water droplets landed on Lana's stomach as he shook his wet hair out. "I'm sure he would if you asked. Although I hear you can buy them for yourself."

"It's not the same. I'd feel more special with fake tits from my husband. How about for our anniversary?"

Ken looked at her incredulously. "I can't tell if you're being serious or not."

"What? No."

Before Ken could open his mouth again, a young voice pealed through the patio.

"Mr. Andrews!" Chloe scuttled out in her flats, waving a package in the air. "The mail came and this was rushed to you!"

Ken tossed his towel aside, bestowing Chloe with the full force of his muscular figure. The girl stopped dead in her tracks, gaping at him, box hanging at her side.

"The package?" Ken asked, holding his hand out.

"Oh, yeah." Finally, Chloe stepped forward. Ken snatched the package from her as if it were nothing.

He turned away from Lana and inspected his mail. His wife, meanwhile, sat up and kicked her legs over the side of her chair. "That'll be all, Chloe," she said curtly. "I'm sure you have other things to be doing." *And one of those things is not staring at my husband's body.* That was Lana's job around those parts.

"No, wait a second, please." Ken motioned for Chloe to come to him, where they conspired about something over by the bushes. *What the?* Lana jumped up, snatching her husband's towel from its lounge chair and wrapping it around her body.

Just as she was about to descend upon husband and help, Ken shoved the package in Chloe's hands and practically shoved her toward the house.

"You know where to leave it," he hissed.

Lana stopped. *Oh hell no.* She watched Chloe scurry back into the mansion as if her ass were lit in an inferno.

"What was all that about? What was in the package?"

Ken wrapped a wet arm around her shoulders. *Fuck off, this bathing suit isn't supposed to get wet.* She didn't dare say that out loud. Her husband would take that as an invitation to toss her into the pool.

"Nothing important, Bunny." His kiss to her cheek was facetious at best. "Boring shit for work that should've been sent to the downtown office."

Lana narrowed her brows as her husband slipped back into the pool and performed some languid backstrokes in the sunlight. *If it were for work, he wouldn't have talked about it with Chloe.* That girl was so low on the staff totem pole that neither Ken nor Lana would talk more than five seconds to her. And that would be to give the order. Not... whatever Ken was saying to her in such a low voice that Lana never had a chance of hearing.

Cynthia Dane

There was something funny going on in her house. Before, Lana drank herself into an afternoon stupor out of irrational fears. Now she wondered if those fears were rational after all.

If they were, then Ken could say goodbye to everything. He could get away with a lot of shit, but cheating on his wife – let alone falling in love with some nobody like *Chloe* – would mean his imminent downfall.

"I'll get to the bottom of this," Lana mumbled, heading back into the house. First, a mimosa on the balcony upstairs. She could better admire her husband's athleticism from there. It may very well be the last time she bothered before the messiest divorce of the decade.

Chapter 4

"Show Her No Mercy."

The windshield wipers squeaked against the glass as the car ascended the next hill. Lana opened her compact, a light glaring against her mirror and preventing her from touching up her lipstick.

Just as well, for Ken hit the same pothole he always hit every time they went into the mountains.

"That was almost a disaster," Lana said, putting her compact and lipstick back in her purse. "One of these days I'll learn that you barely know how to drive."

Ken turned the high beams back on after passing another car. "And yet you let me drive you everywhere. And have yet to divorce me."

He was being facetious, but Lana didn't have much patience for it. "Just don't kill us before we can get laid."

"I love how you always speak of us as a single unit."

"Why not? Everyone else does." Lana wasn't immune to the comments she heard around the club and other social spheres. Everyone called them "the Andrews" because Lana very conveniently changed her name after getting married. *What woman wouldn't?* She heard all the feminist reasoning to, ironically, hang on to her father's last name, but when you were born Lana Losers, you changed your last name when you married whether the man was named Griswold or Habbernacky.

Lana Giselle Andrews. She glanced at herself in the rearview mirror and patted the top of her bun. *That's what I look like.* The more she thought about divorce recently, the more she wondered what she would do about her name. Besides keep it, of course. Wouldn't that get confusing? Sure, it was lazy and convenient to stay Andrews. She could always change it in her next marriage, if there was one.

Funny. She thought about divorce, she even though about her husband remarrying and shrugging over it, but the *thought* of remarrying a brand new man? *I would spend the rest of my life comparing him to Ken.* Lana glanced at her husband. Ken was absorbed in his own world of staying on the road.

They were heading up to Le Château, a destination of theirs regardless of the time of year or how they felt deep inside. In fact, Lana would go as far as to say they were the biggest regulars at the local BDSM brothel. *Excuse me. House of pleasure.*

A Fragile Wife

How long had it been since Lana first exchanged money for kinky services? A year? It was the natural course of her marriage. When they first heard about the Château opening up not so long ago, they talked at length about what they wanted out of it. A cursory inspection told them that it was tasteful, safe, and discreet. A more thorough exam revealed that the girls working there were professionals of the chameleon variety. They could be any type of woman you paid them to be. Dommes, subs, sweet, sassy, bratty... if a man or discerning woman wanted nothing more than a warm hole to make love to, that could be arranged behind the scenes as well. Of course, on paper, the women there only traded dirty words and smacks of the whip for money and gifts. Intercourse and cock sucking were off the record.

Ken and Lana were *so* off the record by now that their mistress Grace knew exactly what to expect. While not expecting anything at all, because Lana was always thinking up something new to do.

They arrived shortly before eight, when the real parties began at the Château. Indeed, two other guests were there, although Lana did not recognize their cars out front. Nor did she garner anything from the coats hanging up in the front hall, where Grace came to meet them for their appointment.

"Let me take that for you, Madam," she said sweetly, running her hands across Lana's shoulders before ripping off her coat. "It's so good to see you once again."

My husband's tastes in action. Ken picked this girl out for them months ago, and since then he and his wife became her primary patrons, a title bestowed upon only the lucky few. Being Grace's patrons meant they could monopolize her time, take her out on dates like to the club, and expect certain services to always be available. Like sex. Lots and lots of sex that Grace did not always give freely to other clients who purchased her services.

Grace could not look more different from Lana, however. For one, she had long, coarse dark hair she always kept parted to one side. She was petite, with thin legs propped up by stiletto heels and a waist that made men salivate and women seethe in jealousy. Her breasts were about the same size as Lana's, but sported tiny brown nipples whereas Lana admired her own thick, pink ones that her husband could never stop sucking when they made love in a position that allowed it. *He rarely sucks her nipples as much.* Lana smiled at the thought as she accepted her usual glass of Chardonnay from Grace's lithe hands.

Hands that gave amazing, *fantastic* massages.

"The Cigar Lounge is currently open," Grace said, heading toward the grand staircase. "Unfortunately the other private rooms for socializing are full tonight."

"Ugh. No." Lana refused to take the first step. "It's bad enough my husband puffs on that electronic shit. I don't need to marinate in the stench of other men's filthy habits."

Ken rolled his eyes. "It's called olfactory fatigue, Lana. You won't notice it soon enough."

"That's what you always say, *Kenneth,* and then the next thing I know I'm gagging until I puke."

Grace tried one of her easy smiles on them. "All right. No Cigar Lounge. Shall we go straight to my room?" Well, *someone* was antsy to start the threesome.

"The Receiving Room is open, Grace," came a voice from behind. Monica Graham stood outside the room in question as another woman escorted an elderly gentleman to the front door. "Please, Mr. and Mrs. Andrews, have a drink with me."

Never let it be said that Monica Graham didn't know how to keep her frequent clients happy. Hardly a visit went by without the madam of the Château bestowing the couple with her company. Not that Lana ever complained. She appreciated a segue into the fuckfest that was their usual visit to the Château.

Grace served them all in the Receiving Room, a quaint corner furnished with Victorian wares reupholstered to look more "sophisticated grandmother" than "dusty ol' shit from the attic." At least the place was well insulated, making it a toasty warm haven for those wanting to have quiet conversations.

"Place looks busy tonight," Ken said to Monica the moment they sat down. "Business must be better than ever."

"We can hardly keep up."

Lana settled on the loveseat between her husband and the mistress. Grace poured a glass of ice water and offered it to Lana, but she declined. "The girls must be kept busy." She glanced at Grace, who didn't flinch or say a word. She merely served, as she was paid to do right now. "Or have you hired more?"

"Not yet." Monica leaned back in her chair, crossing her legs and finally letting go of her rigid stance. While nobody in that room would say they were *friends,* they got along well enough. Monica probably felt a kindred spirit in Lana, even though they were on opposite ends of the Dom/sub spectrum. While Lana considered herself a switch with a more Domme-like public persona, Monica was a lifestyle submissive through and through. She was even the fiancée of lifestyle Dom Henry Warren, a man Ken and Lana did frequent business with. In exchange, they were not charged extra for the double-patronage of Miss Grace, even though Monica was well within her right to milk more money out of the rich Andrews.

Lana didn't chat with lifestyle subs much. Monica was different. She was also a shrewd businesswoman who made her own money independent of her wealthy fiancé. That Lana could respect wholeheartedly.

She also liked her. And after seeing her perform with Henry Warren at the club a few times… well, maybe she had a sexual crush on her as well. *I couldn't give her what she wants, though.* Neither could Ken. Not even the two of them together could satiate the kind of submissive appetite Monica Graham had.

"How is the wedding coming along?" Lana asked, afraid to let the silence continue. Grace got up, turned the corner of the sofa, and stood behind her patrons. One hand snaked across Lana's shoulder while the other stroked the back of Ken's neck. *Good girl.* Lana had to contain a smile of pleasure. "I hear it's going to be the event of the season."

"Just what I need. More pressure." Monica politely looked away as Grace's hand descended Lana's chest and stroked her through her red turtleneck. Pretty little fingers played with the pendant hanging around Lana's neck. *Ken gave me this pendant for my birthday last year.* It was a gold finch, Lana's favorite bird.

She looked at her husband, currently enjoying his glass of scotch and another woman's hand combing through his hair.

Grace knew how to please them, that was for sure. For the past few months she had learned the idiosyncrasies of her patrons and put them to her advantage. Example: she knew that they got off on being treated as one sexual unit. So she always, *always* made sure to show them an equal amount of attention.

Even so, Lana spent most of that night staring at her husband being felt up by another woman. For the first time in a long while, she felt a pang of jealousy. *Fuck that bullshit.* She looked back at Monica and said, "I suppose it's the price you pay for marrying one of the most eligible bachelors in the region." She placed her hand on Ken's arm. "That would've been my Kenny if I let him stay single for much longer."

"That's right. You've been married what, ten years?"

"Yes. Coming up." Lana removed her hand and shrugged Grace's off. "A Christmas wedding for our families. Nothing on the scale of what you have planned." Anyone who was anyone was going to Monica's wedding that upcoming February. At least she was the type of woman who could handle the pressure. Especially if her Dom commanded it so. "Seems quaint to look back on it."

"I'm sure it was lovely."

"She wore a red and white garter," Ken chimed in, stealing a glance at his wife. "The most beautiful white gown any man has ever seen. Cheeky of her to wear something Christmassy beneath it. Felt like unwrapping the most perfect gift."

Lana looked away, hiding her blush. *It wasn't even my idea.* It was her sister's, insisting that she do *something* festive for her wedding clothes. *I only cared about the cake and the sex that night.* Ken had not disappointed her. He took her in ways she didn't know a husband could take his wife – all while making her feel so incredibly loved that she swooned all through their honeymoon.

"I can only hope to have such a grand marriage as you two have." Monica's smile was genuine, although still demure as was her nature. "You're practically legends."

Neither of them pressed for a reason. Having someone young and nubile like Grace feel them up while they spoke was enough reason on display.

"Thank you," Ken finally said. "No marriage is perfect or easy, but Lana and I make it work." His hand curled over her crossed knee. "I can't imagine having anyone else by my side."

Those words would usually make her blush more, but Lana suddenly entered a moment of self-doubt. *Those sound like stock words, Kenneth.* Did her husband hide those kinds of words up his sleeve to use when it was best? Like now? There was a reason some people in the real estate world called him Silver Tongue Andrew. He knew how to charm the pants off a snake. *He's charmed mine off enough times by now.*

Monica couldn't spend much more time with them, not with a busy business bustling with life that night. After she paid her respects and whispered something curt in Grace's ear, Monica saw herself out.

"And how are you, Kitten?" Ken asked, turning every ounce of attention to the mistress. "It's unfortunately been a couple of weeks since we last chatted."

Grace wrapped her arms around his shoulders and bent down low to his ear. Yet she spoke loud enough for Lana to hear as well. "Anything that may have been bothering me is now nothing, sir. A visit from you and your lovely wife is all I need to feel better."

"And the other men you've fucked in our absence?"

Lana could never help herself.

Grace stood up, unfazed. She was probably used to Lana's inquisitions by now. "None of them compare to Mr. Andrews, ma'am."

Liar. Grace slept with a good number of men. Even if not now, at least through her life. So for her to pretend that Ken was the best dick of her life was more than absurd. *I'll take her saying I'm the best woman, though.*

Yet Ken was placated, his male ego stroked as well as his cock usually was. "You're always so crude, Lana," he gently reprimanded. "If I don't mind other men touching our Kitten, then you shouldn't either."

"Who said I minded? It's your dick, dear."

His hand tightened on her knee. "Lana."

"What?" She feigned ignorance with the best of them. "It's the 21st century. Who said a woman had to be confined to one cock? Or a man to one pussy, for that matter?"

"Nobody. You're the one inferring things."

Lana closed her lips before they had an altercation in front of the mistress. That didn't mean Ken won the argument.

"Bunny," her husband said, growling into her ear while Grace looked on. "You're tense. Luckily you're in the perfect place for releasing those urges you're holding in." He leaned back again. "What will make you feel good, my love? You've got your pick tonight."

"I do, don't I?" Lana glanced at Grace, who waited for an order. "Get over here, Kitty. I want to pet you."

Only Lana could make a phrase like that *not* sound cheesy and lame, as evident when Grace responded with alacrity. She stood in front of Lana, hands folded in front of her as she tried to contain a smile. *A liar would say she doesn't like spending time with us.* Grace didn't put up with their whims and demands simply because of the money. Lana guessed the mistress hadn't faked an orgasm since they started this mutually beneficial relationship almost a year ago.

"Kneel."

Lana sat up straight while Grace obeyed and Ken looked on, hand still on his wife's knee. "I knew you were in that sort of mood tonight," he murmured into her ear. "I had hoped."

I know. Ken, like his wife, was a switch. One of the only male switches Lana knew, let alone one of the only male switches who encouraged his partner to be as domineering as possible. *That's one of the things I love about him.* Not ashamed. Never embarrassed. Ken loved exploring even the strangest kinks, even if he decided he didn't like them afterward. Even on the rare occasion something flubbed during sex, like coming too soon, going flaccid for no reason, or saying something to kill the mood indefinitely, Ken didn't let it get to him. It probably helped that his wife didn't care either. *Men go soft. They come. They say stupid shit thinking it's sexy when in reality you want to kill them for saying it.*

So for her husband to sit there, commenting on his wife's growing dominance around another woman, told her everything she needed to know about this situation.

"Show me your tits."

Lana curled her fingers over the edge of the sofa as Grace pulled down the front of her little black dress and showed them the goods they'd seen a million times. Sure enough, those tiny brown dots she called nipples were there – and hardly excited to say hello.

"You don't look excited for us to be here," Lana said, bathing in the attention her husband gave her. "What's going on with those little nubs of yours? Make them hard."

Grace bowed her head and inspected her own nipples. "I don't know why, ma'am. I always look forward to your visits."

"Do you think I give a shit? Those nipples are soft and I want them hard. Get to *it*."

Her husband's hand had a death grip on her knee. When she covertly slipped her hand between his legs, she discovered him half erect already.

"Yes, ma'am."

While Grace deferred to Lana and stimulated herself, the woman in charge pretended to be disinterested to keep up her Domme façade. In truth, she was interested. In everything.

Grace was becoming aroused before her very eyes. Not to mention her husband, who would be on the verge of wanting to do them both within a few more minutes. As for Lana? She came here expecting kinky sex. She was wet when she walked through the front door.

"Look at this slut, Kenneth," Lana said, squeezing her husband's cock. "I don't know how we're not bored with her yet. We've taken her every which way. The both of us."

"Thank you for the reminder."

Yeah, I bet you needed it. Lana rarely knew how a night at the Château would turn out. Sometimes she came in with whips blazing, pushing both her husband and mistress around in an attempt to cuckold them both. Other times she begged for Ken to fuck both her and Grace as if they were nothing to him. Once in a blue moon they both took Grace at the same time – and once, when Ken was one of the most relaxed his wife had ever seen him, he let her peg him in front of someone else. *It's a good thing we pay this woman to be silent.* Not that half the kink scene didn't know the Andrews took it in all their holes from each other, but still…

"You keep her around because you like her, Bunny." Ken kissed his wife's throat. "I picked her out with you in mind."

True. Ken had his fill of the mistress first, months ago. It had been a kink of theirs for some time, and when the Château opened, it seemed like the perfect time to fulfill the fantasy. When the announcement came that Monica was hosting an opening weekend for prospective patrons to get to know the girls, Lana practically demanded that her husband go up and try one out. It was one of the only times they had sex with others separately.

Lana was not surprised when she met Grace. She was everything she liked in a submissive woman. In fact, she was informed by multiple sources that Grace was a natural submissive, whereas other girls at the Château preferred to dominate. Lana didn't need that competition. If she were getting a mistress with her husband, then that young woman's job was to be their *toy*.

Young, perky, obedient, and willing to take whatever they threw at her. If Lana wasn't careful, Grace would end up falling in love with them both. Bad enough they had rented her for the weekend more than once to keep her chained up in their bedroom, ready to serve either one of them whenever they wanted. *Those are wild weekends.*

Now, however, she only had one thing in mind.

"What do you think, Husband? Is she pretty enough?"

The growl vibrating against her skin was so animalistic that she nearly feared Ken turning her over on the couch and fucking her right there. *That's not allowed in here, Kenny. We need to go upstairs.* "You both are," he said.

"I'm talking about her, though." Lana gestured to the breasts on display before them. "Do you want to fuck those tits? Don't think I'd mind seeing you come all over them."

Grace sucked in her breath, which only made her breasts more prominent.

"Or maybe I'll do it first. Push this girl over and come all over her skin. Would you like to see that?"

"I want to see whatever you want, dearest."

"Hmph." Lana shook him off her and stood. "Cover yourself up, Kitty," she said to Grace. "Before you make my husband pop."

"I would never."

"You would," Lana snapped. "I wouldn't hold it against you, though. Just save one for me."

Grace pulled her bust up and led her patrons from the Receiving Room. The staircase was only a few feet away, and by the time they reached the second floor, Ken already had his arm completely around Lana's torso.

"Show at ten," he muttered, nodding toward an open door.

He wasn't kidding. There, on full display, was another young woman tied up in her bed, a man in a black mask smacking a crop against her pussy and forcing orgasms out of her. *Did he pay extra to keep her door open?* A man after Lana's exhibitionist heart.

Grace waited outside her room, smiling as she unlocked the door. "For you two, I'll leave the door open for no extra charge."

"That's right, sweetie," Lana said, putting her hand on Grace's shoulder and teasing her cheek with hot breath. Feeling this woman, who couldn't be more than fifteen years her junior, shudder beneath her stature made Lana wetter. "You don't charge us for lots of shit you should. I bet your madam loves that."

Grace held a finger to her lips. "What Madam Monica doesn't know…"

"Don't be coy, Kitten." Ken helped himself into the bedroom. "We know there are cameras in here. Why do you think my wife always gets fucked in the same spot?" He stopped in front of Grace's king-sized bed. "She wants to make sure the cameras capture her best angle."

"It's true. In another life I would've been a porn star." Probably.

The door was closed behind them. The moment it latched, Lana drew Grace into her arms and kissed her pretty lips.

"That didn't take long," Ken said, sitting on the edge of the bed. He removed his jacket and tossed it onto the nearest bench. "You have a good appetite tonight, Wife."

Lana let her lips linger on Grace's before shoving her back. "I bet you'd like to watch me with her, huh?" She yanked one of the dress straps down Grace's arm, a hint of those nipples – hard, this time – coming into view.

"I don't mind watching you fuck almost anyone."

That was a lie. They joked that Ken was omnisexual, but he still got his rocks off hardest over two women going at it. He may have picked out Grace because he knew his wife would like her, but it wasn't like *Ken* didn't like her either. He often dropped hints that he liked watching them have fun together. *At least I know what to get him for his birthday.* Earlier that year she treated her husband to a full lesbian Dom/sub show, complete with strap-on in every hole it could go. Grace earned her session bonus ten times over that night.

"At least our kitty is hot." Lana finished undressing their mistress, not surprised to find no underwear on the girl. When the dress dropped to the floor, Grace was completely naked, her flat, toned stomach the envy of the one other woman in the room. *It just makes me want to fuck her harder.* No. Not tonight.

Lana had other plans.

She looked at her husband, who watched in mild amusement. *Fuck this harlot.* She said as much with her narrow eyes, burrowing deep into Ken's wide ones. *I wanna see you fuck her until you nearly come.*

Such thoughts had swam in Lana's head since the last time she drank on her office floor, wondering if her husband was banging the maid behind his wife's back. It would be easy enough to do in their big home. Chloe had full run, being the only full-time maid they employed. The amount of opportunities Ken had to lure the girl away, lift her skirt, and fuck her were numerous.

Yet Lana didn't consider herself a *jealous* woman. She couldn't be, with the kind of marriage she had. Ken fucked other people in front of her. She fucked other people in front of him. Sometimes even in public, although they preferred to keep it private. Everyone knew that Ken and Lana Andrews flirting with them meant they were interested in some group fun. *It's one of the reasons I married him.* Lana couldn't be confined to one man for the rest of her life. She needed to flirt, to grab, and to even full-on sexually satisfy and be satisfied by other men from time to time. Women, too. She was hesitant to label herself bisexual since she had no interest in a serious relationship with a woman like she did with men, but it was true. Women like Grace aroused her.

I thought I hit the jackpot with Ken. A man who wasn't afraid to try all manner of things? Who was handsome, good in bed, and would occasionally blow another man for Lana's sole amusement? Shit! Sign her up and put a ring on it!

Her jealousy was only tempered when she was watching, their fantasy over shopping for Grace notwithstanding. Besides, Grace was an exception. Lana actually got off on the idea that her husband was up in these mountains screwing a woman, going through a checklist of things his wife would like.

Chloe was a completely different story. *If* her husband were cheating on her, then he was doing it purely for his own selfishness. He didn't care about her feelings. He was *bored.* That made Lana jealous.

The only way to placate her irrational emotions right now was to watch her husband take this nobody.

Because Grace *was* a nobody compared to Kenneth Andrews's wife. The woman he asked to marry him. The woman he remained married to for ten years. The woman he still looked at with adoration... although it was possible he looked at other women like that too.

Stop it, Lana. She didn't want to be jealous. She wanted to have some *fun.*

"Bend over the bed and spread your legs."

Lana didn't even watch as Grace obeyed, her flat but cute ass shoved in the air as her stiletto heels gave her height over the bed. Lana only had eyes for her husband, who continued to stand nearby as if this whole scenario amused him.

"You're going to fuck her," Lana informed him, fingers pulling apart his shirt, his trousers. "I'm going to watch you fuck this nobody's pussy."

"Yes, ma'am."

"Don't be smart with me." Lana pulled his half erect cock out of his pants, her hand stroking his length. "I don't have the patience for it right now."

Before Ken could test her patience any further, Lana knelt on the floor and practically devoured her husband's cock.

This wasn't foreplay. This was preparing him to fulfill her fantasy of the moment. So there was no lovingly languid way of sucking him, tasting his scent, or playing coy with him. It was purely about getting him hard enough to fuck their mistress.

And hey, if his cock was covered in some of her wetness before it sank into another woman, all the better.

Speaking of… Her husband only deserved the best. And if the best wasn't Lana in that moment, then the best was at least a wet place to thrust his cock. Lana ran her hand up Grace's bare thigh, teasing her entrance before shoving two eager fingers inside. *Get wet, damnit.* Grace groaned into her bed covers, hips meeting the thrusts of Lana's fingers. Once Lana was able to penetrate past the coarse flesh of a woman's entrance and touch the smooth walls beyond, she pulled her fingers out.

And the moment she felt Ken rigid in her mouth and tasted precum on her tongue, Lana backed off.

"Fuck her," she growled in her husband's ear. "Fuck her for *me*."

Ken wrapped his hand around the back of her head and kissed her, his tongue slamming against hers. *No, dumbass, I said fuck her!* Men!

"Yes, ma'am." Ken eased away from his wife, his erection lining up with Grace's spread opening. "Wouldn't want to disappoint you."

Lana stood nearby, arms crossed before her red turtleneck and gold finch necklace. "Show her no mercy, and I won't be disappointed. I want to hear that kitty cry."

Cry Grace did – cried out, her body quickly invaded by another woman's husband.

God strike me dead, this is too hot to bear. Yet Lana would stand there stoically, in case either the mistress or the cuckolding husband glanced in her direction. She was dominant in this situation. She could not waver, even though her body flushed in heat and her pussy begged to have a piece of that action.

Because Ken was a *god* right now.

He took their mistress, thrusting into her over and over, smacking her ass to make her moan and beg. *That's right. Beg for my husband's cock.* Grace spared one second to look over her shoulder at Ken, her face so full of respect for what he could do to her that Lana couldn't help but puff up in pride. *Tell the world how good he is. Then remind them all that I am his wife.* Lana covertly brushed her arm against her breast, feeling the jolts of desire pass through her.

The sweat on her husband's forehead. His rolled up sleeves. His slightly open mouth as he put the full force of his strength into taking this woman they mutually desired. Ken was never as sexy as he was now, when he put his sexual prowess and display to his wife. He could have almost any woman he tried to seduce. They all wanted him, once he got their attention. *But it's me he married.* Lana pulled her sweater out of her black miniskirt so she could push her hand beneath and stroke a nipple.

"That's right," she snarled, leaning down so Grace could hear anything over her cries. Being on the receiving end of Ken's cock had that effect on women. "That's my husband fucking you. How does it make you feel knowing you've given yourself to a married man? Does it make you feel *good?* Does it make you want to come? Do you want him to come inside you?"

Grace shook her head wildly, black hair flinging this way and that as she rode Ken's cock. Did that mean yes or no? Who cared? Lana could have cackled.

"Fuck that pussy, baby." Lana put her hand on Ken's abdomen, feeling his muscles work as he pounded another woman. "Is it as wet as it looks?"

He grunted in the affirmative.

"I knew it. Keep going. I want to see your cum drip out of her cunt." This time she did laugh, taking her turn to spank

Grace's ass. "Because he ain't the first one to do that this month, is he? How many men have you fucked this month?"

Her crazed voice roused Grace from her stupor. Her eyes were still glazed over, but a word managed to sound in the air. "Five!"

"Five? Five men? Goodness, you really are a slut. How many of them came inside you?"

She moaned heavily, her breasts shaking from the impact of Ken's thrusts as she rode out a sudden, quick orgasm. "None of them!" she cried. "I only do that with you!"

"Good answer." That was another perk to being a patron. Condomless sex. *Fill this woman's cunt up with cum, Husband.* "Because my husband is the only man who should get those honors."

Lana was content to watch this play out. The more she thought about her husband claiming this woman, the more she liked the idea. *My virile husband.* How many women could say they had a man as adventurous as hers? Lana was able to forget her jealousy long enough to kiss Ken's cheek and lightly tongue his ear.

She didn't know what she did. Maybe it was the tongue. Maybe it was giving him too much attention. Before she knew it, however, Ken pulled out of Grace and turned on his wife.

"Mmf!" Lana went down on the bed, her skirt hiked up around her waist and her silk underwear tearing toward the floor. Her legs opened on their own accord. The room grew dark as her eyes slammed shut. Her hand smacked against Grace, only a few inches away.

"Shut up." That harsh, domineering command flicked a switch in Lana's brain. She came in here, intent on taking over the room and directing all sexual activity. And now her husband was tossing that plan upside down. "She's not the only loose woman around here."

Oh no, he's speaking my language. Literally. Figuratively.

"Tell me, Lana." Whatever fueled Ken was now fueling Lana, who bent in sexual submission before her master. "Tell me you want it."

She whimpered, aware of how she looked in front of the mistress. *There goes my Domme credibility tonight.* "I want it, sir."

Ken flipped her over, forcing her nose against Grace's wet thigh. The heavy scent of a woman's arousal smacked Lana in the face. *Oh my God.* So heady. So *heady.* The feminine aroma made her even more submissive – although her husband spreading her legs open and stretching her pussy with the head of his cock helped. "Eat her. We're taking you, Lana."

Grace laughed in the background. It had to be the background. Because she was so, so far away.

Whenever this happened – whenever Lana entered her submissive headspace, even if she was whiplashing from the Domme one – she felt no desire to do anything. Except obey.

So when her husband, the man who possessed her as his for all eternity, told her to pleasure another woman, she did it without hesitation.

Yet she knew this was not necessarily for Ken's amusement, although he undoubtedly got off on it. This was about her, even still.

A Fragile Wife

This was about putting her in her place. God knew she needed it.

"Does it taste good?" Ken asked, his cock ready to take his wife as she whimpered against a woman's wet slit. "Can you taste me in her?"

Yes, she could. It was mostly Grace's scent and taste, but Ken had definitely been here recently. After twelve years together, Lana knew his presence.

It made her want to worship the mistress, a woman lucky enough to be bestowed with Ken Andrews's cock. In another few seconds, Lana would be as worthy as well.

"Don't underestimate me, Wife." Ken pushed himself in, the friction from Lana's unusually tight entrance making them both wince. "You may get to have your fun sometimes, but this still belongs to me."

The way he said it filled Lana with the kind of twisted elation that would scare off most women. This man wanted to own her. *Possess* her. Lord over her with the fact he had a cock and she was in love with him. In that moment, she didn't care who he banged on the side. She forgot her petty jealousies that may not have meant anything at all… because Ken had given up the chance to claim the mistress to instead take his wife.

I love him so much.

Even when it hurt. Even when he was so rough with her that she cried out in a mixture of pain and need. *Even* when he shoved her face down into another woman's wetness, forcing her to breathe that scent deeply into her nose as she licked

Grace's slit up and down. The mistress laughed. Laughed at *her* and how quickly she had been put into her place.

Go on. Laugh at me. I'm the one he's fucking.

No, she was the slut now. She was higher in status than Grace, but she was lower in her husband's eyes right now. Did she love it!

"Don't fight my cock," Ken barked, his cock already swelling inside his wife. *Don't come yet, baby. Give me another minute of this!* "Don't you want it, Lana? Don't you want me fucking you like you deserve?"

"I'm not fighting!" She sounded so pathetic, muffled by another woman's body. "Please, sir, I'm not!"

"Then take my cock like the obedient wife you are."

She sobbed, and she wasn't sure why. Was it because her husband took her to that place in front of another woman? If it were going to happen in front of anyone, it would be Grace, their tight-lipped mistress who couldn't judge them even if she wanted. *Besides, she's seen me peg him and call him a sissy.* Nothing was sacred in front of the mistress, not even words like that.

"Yes, sir," Lana finally said. "I'm a bigger whore than this one here."

"Damn straight you are." He pulled out and slammed into her again, opening her up, but barely enough. Luckily, Lana was so aroused that she was wet enough to take whatever he gave her now. "This woman may be a professional, but you married me. You know what that means."

I married you, so I'm the biggest whore of all. They said they went halfsies, but Ken had the biggest advantage. He paid for so much. He gave his wife countless new opportunities by marrying and going into business with her. He gave her credibility with his last name. No matter how Lana spun it, she would always be Ken's biggest whore.

She nearly pulled her own hair out of her scalp from how hot the realization made her.

"Now shut up and take what you deserve."

"Yes, sir."

She was trapped between his harsh cock and the soft woman in front of her. Grace could only watch in fascination as this dynamic unfolded before her. What was she thinking? That these two were certifiably crazy? *We are. Everyone knows it.* That they were the best time she ever had? That she would be paying for a new designer dress with the bonus they would give her... to keep quiet about how Ken Andrews made his ball-busting wife Lana admit she was his biggest whore?

Who cared?

Lana buried her face in Grace, moaning into the welcoming folds of this professional woman as Ken took her deep and raw from behind. Pulsations spread through Lana's abdomen. Her husband's cock swelled in her entrance, threatening to stretch her to limits she normally didn't push. The mistress writhed beneath her mouth, orgasming from the intensity of the situation.

When Ken came, he slammed Lana's hips down onto his cock, burying himself so deep that she had no chance to escape his climax and what it was doing to her. Assuming she wanted to – which she did not.

She wanted to feel his hands pin her down. She *wanted* to feel his cock release the first burst of seed inside her, then the next.

"Please give it all to me," she mumbled into Grace's pussy. Yet she knew he wouldn't.

Sure enough, he quickly pulled out, another burst hitting her ass before Ken could practically shove his cock into Grace's waiting mouth.

He didn't make it that far. The last of his long orgasm hit the mistress's breasts, her eyes rolling back in her head as she collapsed onto the bed.

Lana sank to the floor. Crumpled.

"My two girls," he mused, admiring what he had done to the both of them. "I'm the luckiest man in the world."

Lana braced herself against the bed, her finger circling her clit as she shuddered in the orgasm she couldn't have with her husband inside her. He watched her, wordlessly, as she let loose everything inside her all over the mistress's bedroom floor. *We pay to clean this up.* Might as well get her money's worth.

"And that's why you're my favorite, baby." Ken knelt next to her, stroking her sweaty forehead and patting her back. "Nobody but you knows how to appreciate what I offer."

She looked him in the eye. Although worn out, her pussy too sore to deal with anything else, Lana still managed to say, "Your favorite, huh? Do I want to know who your lessers are?" Against her wishes she thought of Chloe, the young ass who probably got off on calling herself Ken's wench too.

At least I'm his favorite.

Ken didn't answer her. He probably thought she was having post-sex rambles that didn't always make sense.

They spent the night with Grace, opting to drive back home in the morning. The girl's bed was big enough for the three of them. Yet even after Lana washed up and curled into her husband's arms, she couldn't stop fighting the paranoia creeping up on her. The one that told her she was the best, but she wasn't the only one who kept her husband's fancy.

Go away... That's what she told these invasive thoughts. She had no evidence. She only had her paranoia and the feelings that made her so toxic that she couldn't even enjoy the way they made love anymore. Not after the sordid fact.

She held onto her husband and hoped he would find a way to soothe her soon. Before it was too late for their marriage.

Chapter 5

"What Do You Have There?"

For once, Lana was not lying on her office floor, with or without a drink. *Hey, I don't* always *drink down here.* Sometimes she asked Chloe to bring her tea or coffee. *Most* of the time it was tea or coffee. The alcohol only happened when she started thinking darker thoughts, usually brought on because she didn't have enough work to do.

That Thursday, however, she didn't end up on the floor at all. Instead, she had Chloe bring her coffee straight to the desk, where the desktop showed spreadsheets galore.

"Two sugars and a pinch of cream," Chloe announced, setting the sterling silver serving set on the edge of Lana's desk. "Also, if it's okay, I'm going to take my half hour break."

Lana looked away from her financial spreadsheets and caught sight of a suppressed grin on Chloe's face. "You finished your other duties for now?"

"Yes, ma'am."

The lady of the house gestured to the serving set, and with a flourish the young maid poured more coffee into the cup. "Then it's fine."

Chloe excused herself. Lana sighed, sipping her hot coffee and perusing her email. A voice mail from Ken waited on her cell phone. He would be home late again. *I need to postpone dinner until 7:30.* Hopefully Lana would remember to tell Roberta, the live-in chef.

Since she was in a productive mood – it helped that she and Ken were getting ready to remodel a day spa to sell to an expanding company, and thinking about free manipedis and massages *always* got her ass moving – Lana finished work early and decided to take her phone calls outside. Why not? It was an unusually sunny day for that time of year. She needed a light scarf and sweater to brave the chill, but once she was in the sunshine, walking past the pool and into the trails behind the mansion, she couldn't care about the chill.

Her cousin the lawyer called, asking where her weekly gripe about a divorce was. This was followed by another call from Ken saying their current real estate deal went up two million dollars, and, oh, could his dear wife and business partner come with him to negotiations next time? Finally, she got a call from her sister, coordinating their Christmas dinner at their parents' house. Ken's family was coming over... so were the sisters of

Cynthia Dane

Lana's brother-in-law. For the first time in a long while, Lana would be surrounded by children, and she wasn't sure how she felt about that.

No thank you.

She would have to enjoy the peace now. She would also have to summon her driver one of these days and do some last minute Christmas shopping. Especially for those children. *Sigh.*

Toward the end of her stroll, she came upon Chloe, sitting on a bench in the sunlight. This wasn't unusual, since the girl often took her breaks outside on nicer days, but today she held something in her hand.

That something was a large piece of Kenneth's personal stationery. Easy to see that soft yellow even in the sunlight.

Chloe giggled at something written on the paper. Before she saw Lana approaching, the maid covered her mouth as a smile erupted on her stricken face. It was a face of adoration. Love.

Lana knew that face well. It made her stop in her steps and feel bile erupt in her throat. *I knew it.* She looked away as Chloe noticed her, furiously fighting to put the paper away in a purse she kept strapped around her chest.

"What do you have there?" Lana asked sweetly, taking her chances.

Chloe ran her fingers nervously through her hair. "Nothing special," she replied much too quickly. "I mean…"

"Love letter from your boyfriend?"

The fake look of innocence dropped from Chloe's mien. Instead, she paled, the winter sunshine sucking all color from

- 70 -

her face. "I don't have a boyfriend," she finally said. *Yes, sweetie, I saw whose stationery you were perusing. Naughty girl.*

"Too bad. Pretty girl like you should have a boyfriend around Christmas."

"I'm going home to visit my parents anyway."

"Aren't we all?"

Lana took her leave, diverting from the main house to the kitchen wing nestled on the far west side of the property. Roberta was there, prepping ingredients for dinner. Looked like braised chicken and a vegetable medley.

"Ken will be home late," Lana said, standing in front of the island counter stacked with fresh vegetables. Roberta, a stocky woman with a mean visage but a straightforward heart, sliced and diced as if it were second nature. It probably was, like buying and selling properties flowed in Lana's blood. *We all have our strengths.* Wasn't Lana's fault that hers made her one of the richest women in the region – if not *the* richest. Not even fellow billionaire Kathryn Alison had as much money as Lana's personal savings account.

Roberta stopped cutting long enough to consider the food in front of her, then Lana's stoic face. "Gives me longer to cook dessert."

"What's for dessert?"

"Peach cobbler. For Mr. Andrews."

His favorite. Seemed Ken was a popular guy today. "Can I ask you a question?"

Roberta glanced at Lana as if she had grown a second head. *I know, I'm not very personable.* Although Lana tried to keep emotional distance between her and the help she hired, Roberta was the house's longest standing employee at seven years. She lived in a sizable apartment above the kitchen where the Andrews let her host guests and even a live-in boyfriend for three out of those seven years – the boyfriend had worked as a lawn keeper for a neighboring property, meaning hardly any commute. These were perks Lana wouldn't dream of offering her other employees.

So even though Roberta and her were far from *friends,* she was the closest thing Lana had to one in that house outside of her husband. If there was anyone she was going to talk to, it was this sullen woman who often looked like she was about to rip the chicken in half with her bare hands.

"Do you think my husband is cheating on me?"

Lana went ahead and laid that out on the island counter, now didn't she?

Roberta spared her another glance before dumping a pile of diced carrots into a bowl. "It's too close to Christmas for a question like that," she mumbled.

"I'm serious. I think there might be something going on between him and Chloe."

Roberta shrugged. "What evidence do you have of this?"

Classic Roberta. She had no other reaction than, "Evidence? Where's your evidence?" This was why Lana liked her. That and she cooked a mean lasagna.

"I have my reasons for thinking this."

"That means you have no evidence."

Lana huffed. "I caught the girl reading something on my husband's stationery. She was being secretive about it. And giggling over it."

"Okay, but have you seen them together like that? Has either of them said anything?"

"Well, no…"

Roberta shrugged again. "If you're worried, fire the girl."

"That doesn't solve my problems." Ken would find someone else to fool around with. Probably in the city where Lana would never find out. "Besides, it's such a pain in the ass hiring live-in maids around here. I have to take applications, interview them, give them trial runs… Chloe's only been here a few months. I don't want to go through that again if I don't have to." Obviously, if Chloe were screwing the boss's husband, then she would have to *go*.

"Your problems sound like they're in your head."

Lana could have responded in any number of ways. She could have yelled at Roberta. Could have fired her on the spot for saying such a thing. Could have sent a warning shot with her sharp, biting tongue.

Instead, Lana said, "You're right. They are. Except my instincts have brought me this far in my life, and my instincts say that there's *something* going on. Something is being kept from me in this house."

"Well, I know nothing about it, ma'am." Roberta waved her knife around for emphasis. "But if you do find out that the bastard is cheating on you, know that I can slip any ol' thing into his chicken soup. Like a shitton of laxatives, if you know what I mean."

"I think I get your point." As amusing as it would be to destroy the man's colon for a day or two, Lana wasn't sure what that would accomplish. "I appreciate your candor, as always."

"That's why you come to me."

"Indeed." Lana turned, shoulders square and ponytail pulling tight against her scalp. "Let me know if you notice anything, though."

Before she could step out of the kitchen, Roberta called out, "There was one thing, ma'am."

Lana stopped. "Oh? Do tell."

"This is conjecture on my part, but maybe it will mean something to you."

"Please, go on."

Roberta looked around the kitchen, as if anyone but her, Lana, and the deliveryman who brought the food three times a week ever came in there. "The other day when I was serving Mr. Andrews breakfast, I saw him pull the maid aside and whisper something into her ear. It was not work related, ma'am. The girl was blushing like crazy and your husband looked fairly pleased with himself." Roberta caught her words. "More so than usual."

"I see. Is that all?"

"No."

Lana braced herself.

"He then asked her if she would meet him in his office for something personal on a day you went shopping in town. They were in there for two hours. I had to clean the whole dining room by myself, so I gave her a bit of an earful on your behalf."

Well, that was certainly *not* something Lana wanted to hear. Nevertheless, she thanked Roberta again and wandered off to consider this information and what it possibly meant.

Ken and Chloe definitely had *something* going on. Lana could confront her. She could pull that maid aside and demand a confession. Yet what good would that do? All Lana would do was scare her into either quitting or lying. *And Ken would keep on keeping on.*

Ken.

Her fucking husband.

If the bastard were cheating on her, then getting rid of Chloe wouldn't do a damn thing. And if he were cheating? That was it. That was the final breaking point. He thought it was cute to bug her about calling for a divorce, but he didn't know the full fury of Lana Andrews, a woman he helped create over the past decade.

I mean, he has every opportunity to explore his sexuality with other people. The deal was it happened with Lana present and with her consent. Ken going off secretly with people, keeping his wife in the dark, was such a breach of trust that Lana was certain she could never recover from it.

If Ken were cheating on her, their marriage was over. No buts. No forgiveness.

Cynthia Dane

I don't want that… Lana stood in the front hall of the mansion she bought with her husband years ago. This was her home. This was her past, her present, and hopefully her future. Why would she give this up unless she really had to?

She no longer flippantly thought of a divorce to mix things up in her life. That was absurd. First she had to find out if her fears were for naught or a reality. Until then, she would assume that everything was fine. Lana was good at separating emotions like that. The next time she saw her husband, she would pretend that nothing was amiss. Although her eyes would try to see all, and her ears would be on top of everything.

Ken was going to come home to the nosiest wife in the universe.

Chapter 6

"You Wouldn't Understand."

"There she is," Lana said, relieved. She flagged down someone on the other side of the main room of The Dark Hour, the elite BDSM club she and Ken were regulars at.

"Finally, she has a friend." Ken teased his wife, but he wasn't far off the mark. Lana didn't have many people she considered herself *close* with. Ken was her best friend, all things considered. She got along with her sister, but Inid was one of the most vanilla women in the world when it came to sex and gender expression. The other women Lana knew in her social circle were often put off by her brash mannerisms. There were few women, usually Dommes, who could put up with Lana's brand of socializing for more than ten minutes.

Elle Hernandez was one such woman.

Cynthia Dane

She approached, sashaying like a goddess in her white miniskirt and the gold chains hanging from her long neck. Big, bold and brown hair fell in curly waves, caressing the woman's tanned skin

"Lana!" They exchanged kisses before sitting in their corner of the VIP lounge. Leather stretched and creaked beneath them as they rearranged their bodies and said their pleasantries. Ken gave them some privacy and spoke with an acquaintance on the neighboring couch.

"It's so good to see you around," Lana said. "It's been much too long."

"Two months. Chicago has been keeping me busy." Elle halved her time between their city and Chicago, although she spent most of her time in Chicago those days. "I'm home for the holidays. Too bad, because I would rather hang out here than spend my time at my mother's."

"Ain't that the truth?" Christmas was a little over a week away. This would probably be the last busy night for The Dark Hour until the New Year's party. Even Lana, who finally made Christmas present arrangements for her extended family, was starting to pack for her and her husband's trip upstate in the coming days.

"How are things? Still kicking ass and taking names?"

"Of course." Lana flagged a server and ordered a double of what she already had. "I wouldn't have my life any other way. Someone around here has to represent the pussy-having business side of things."

Elle laughed. "If I had half the business tenacity that you do, I would probably join you in that. As it is, I can barely balance personal and public. I haven't dated anyone in three months. Hoping I can score some ass tonight."

Lana looked around the room. "I think you'll have your choice of studs." On a busy night, there were always unpaired male subs wandering around, looking for a boot to lick and a strap-on to ride. Or somewhere in between. Elle was a popular Domme who usually had her pick of them. Something Lana quickly brought up before her friend could change subjects.

"I hear it's even easier now. Dommes pairing off left and right, leaving us singles with all the hard cock we can swallow."

"'Tis been a big year for romance in the kink scene, that's for sure." Even if old, established couples broke up, new ones popped up to take their places.

Two of them came by now, since Ken couldn't contain himself and invited them over the moment he spotted them.

"Lana," Ian Mathers, dressed as if he came from a meeting said in acknowledgment. His recently cut hair was striking in the dim lights of the club, but nowhere near as striking as his arm candy, the filthy rich and beautiful Kathryn Alison. The two of them were a fellow switch couple, although from Lana's bored understanding, Kathryn did more submitting than her boyfriend. Tonight, however, nobody had a collar or leash on, and Kathryn greeted Elle Hernandez with a big, vibrant smile and a loud voice. Apparently they knew each other well.

Lana was always in the mood to talk to more likeminded women. Elle was great, but adding Kathryn the dominating woman was even better. Too bad Kathryn didn't think much of Lana, or so the wife of Ken Andrews surmised. Their conversations were often tenuous at best. For all her bravado, Kathryn didn't care much for Lana's flirty personality. Or something. Lana wasn't absolutely sure, nor did she care.

Tonight Kathryn was pleasant company as the men and women segregated themselves to talk Christmas, business plans for the new year, and sex. Not necessarily in that order.

Lana was in the middle of describing the sex swing she and Ken were thinking about installing in their playroom when Ian came over, tapped on his girlfriend's shoulder, and whispered something into her ear. They exchanged smiles before Kathryn was sucked into an ongoing conversation on the boys' side about her father's current plans for a property he purchased in another state.

"So how's the swinging," Elle asked, leaning in toward Lana. "And I don't mean the sex swing. Or maybe I do?"

"Things are the same," Lana responded. She didn't feel like bringing up her suspicions. After all, she came to one of her favorite places to relax and think about anything *but* a cheating husband. Even if she came with that husband. And even if she planned on screwing that husband sometime tonight. *Wouldn't be a night at The Dark Hour without fucking my husband.* The only question was whether she would Top or bottom.

"Maybe you should try those two tonight," Elle teased, motioning to Ian and Kathryn. "They seem fun."

"Hardly," Lana muttered into her drink.

"I thought you used to crush on Mathers."

A Fragile Wife

"I've crushed on a lot of men, Elle."

"I seem to recall you specifically saying that you wanted to suck his cock."

"I was drunk."

"The shit you say when you're drunk is what you're thinking 24/7 anyway."

Lana laughed. "All right, you caught me. I *used* to think that about him." Honestly, that germ was planted by Ken. Lana garnered that her husband had a man-crush of his own.

"What changed? Him getting a girlfriend couldn't have deterred you. Even if you and Ken weren't omnipanquasisexuals you'd still hit on Mathers."

Cute. Elle didn't mean any harm by such a comment, but sometimes Lana got tired of defending her lifestyle, even to friends. Yes, she would've kept flirting with Ian until he told her to permanently back off. Wouldn't be the first time a man did that, to either her or Ken. No, the reason Lana lost interest was much more petty.

"I thought he'd be fun until I got a glimpse of his cock."

"Uh oh." Elle's smile was beyond ludicrous, as if they were having a sleepover as teenagers. Where were the pillows and Boyz II Men CDs? "He got a tiny buddy?" Elle was not covert at all when she glanced over at Ian Mathers, eyes pointed straight at his dick. "I mean... can't see much from here..."

"No," Lana said, lowering her voice. "It's sort of the opposite problem."

"Oh, *girl.*"

"Shut up. I ain't saying he's got a monster cock. I'm saying I took one look at it and crossed my legs." Sometimes it was hard being a woman like her. Fact of the matter was, the only intimidating thing about Ian's dick was his abnormally large tip. It wasn't *huge*, but big enough to make Lana think twice about going through all the effort necessary to seduce him – and, by extension, his girlfriend.

"Life is so hard sometimes." Elle sighed. "I can't say I ever thought about him. Not really my type, if you know what I mean. I like my men more... pliable." After a hearty laugh, she continued, "You going to take your handsome husband to task for something tonight? I wouldn't mind watching some hot Domme and male sub action. Knowing this place..." She looked around the room, including the empty performance stage. "It'll be a Dom fest. It always is when the Dommes aren't scheduled in advance."

"I could as easily say that to you. Find some stud and jerk him off for us."

"Not in the mood. I'd rather watch a fun couple like you guys."

Lana shook her head. "Don't think we'll be doing that tonight. Sorry."

"Oh, well. A woman can always try."

Normally Lana's exhibitionism would certainly drive her to asking her husband to perform together on stage. They had done it before, countless times by this point. Most of the people in this room had seen his cock, her pussy, and what they looked like when they met for a bit of a lay. *I don't give a shit.*

Nobody in this place has any room to judge. She had seen a fair number of these cocks and cunts herself. *Haven't seen Kathryn's. Bet she shaves.* No. Waxed.

Lana remembered she was due for a spa day. It had been a while since she went for a body wax. Maybe that could be a Christmas surprise for Ken.

I bet that Chloe goes all natural. Ken claimed to have no preference, but for Lana, someone who enjoyed grooming herself from top to bottom, being cast aside for someone on the other end of the spectrum would be like an extra kick to her gut. It would have felt the same if she were the "all natural" one and Chloe was gifted all the waxes she could stand.

"Lana?"

She came back to reality, where her husband joined her on the couch and the others went their separate ways. Elle remained a few more minutes before excusing herself to go cruise for a sub. Once they were alone, Lana sank against her husband, smelling his intense scent and reminding herself that they came here to have fun.

"How's my Bunny?" He slapped his hand against her knee and drew a circle against her skin. "Have a nice chat with your friend?"

"I could ask you the same thing."

"It was a good conversation. Always nice to catch up with people. What were you and Elle talking about?"

Lana leaned against the back of the couch and stared at the gray wall behind it. "Ian Mathers's cock."

"Ah."

"I don't expect you to understand."

"Now, now, Bunny, I like to consider myself a fair expert on all things dick and cock. So I definitely understand."

She glanced at him. "Not from my tight pussy's perspective."

"So we don't flirt with him anymore. We find someone else to take for a spin." Ken snorted. "He's got a serious girlfriend now anyway. They're so smitten with each other, it's almost adorable. Hopefully they won't be like us old harpies one day."

It took a few seconds for that to sink into Lana's ear. "What do you mean, *old?*"

"Good. She's listening to her husband for once."

Lana clasped her hands around his arm and nearly nibbled on the bottom of his ear. "Maybe it's you who should be listening to me."

"Shh." He patted her knee. "There's a show starting. We should watch."

His gentle voice was the only thing in the world that could placate her personality. Whether she was wound up in anger or lust, sometimes she needed to come down from her adrenaline-pumping high and remember her place in the world. Right now, that place was being a responsible and socially acceptable woman in a sex club.

That meant giving the stage her rapt attention as a man in a black silk shirt and trousers stepped up with a woman attached to a leash.

"This should be good," Ken said, asking for a refill of his drink from a server. "Care to wager about what they do?"

"Always, Kenny." Lana bit her lip in anticipation. "Loser has to give the other a hand-job right here."

"Done. What do you wager?"

"I say he fucks her within five minutes. They look eager."

"Five minutes? That quick? You're on. I give it at least five." Ken held up his wrist and waited for the second hand to hit twelve. "Starting now."

That didn't give Lana much leeway. The Dom and his sub were barely set up when Ken started his countdown, but there was one thing on Lana's side.

Both of them were young – not only the girl. Most female subs tended to gravitate toward older, experienced Doms. Certainly, the young man may have had plenty of experience in the kink scene so far. *I doubt it.* That meant Mr. College Dom would constantly be on the verge of losing it. That *it?* The very thing that made the more experienced Doms in the room attractive.

Discipline.

Men like Ken – hell, like any Dom over thirty in that room – knew how to hold back their need to take their delicate subs. Their discipline was one way to feel immense pleasure. So, all Lana had to count on was this young lad's dick getting so hard he couldn't help but reward even the brattiest sub with it.

Ken sensed this as well the moment the show started. He sighed deeply, resigned to probably losing. Although the watch was ticking.

"He's good looking," he said wistfully, hand stroking his wife's knee. "Wouldn't mind seeing you take him on."

That was Ken's casual way of suggesting Lana have her turn with a third wheel. A male one. "We'll see how I feel about that soon enough." To say they used these more explicit shows as a way to shop for potential playmates was an understatement. Both Lana and Ken wanted to see how other people screwed – or, in Lana's case, see the goods they were packing.

Sure enough, the guy's dick was out in fewer than three minutes. Erect. *Looks painful.* Lana didn't have a dick, but she could guess. Just like she could guess Ken crossing his legs had nothing to do with phantom pains. The man was 100% hiding his own erection.

"If this guy can hold on two more minutes, Kenny, I'll take care of that thing for you."

"I know you will, Bunny."

He kissed her hand as the Dom spanked his sub, pulled down her bust, and fondled her modest breasts. *Wouldn't mind getting a taste of that right now.* Whether from Ken or another man while her husband watched… that didn't matter.

"How long do you think they've been together?" Lana asked. She couldn't believe it being more than a few months. These two were too young to have a longstanding Dom/sub relationship. Not like her and Ken. "I would guess three months, tops."

"Five weeks."

"That's specific."

"Long enough for that guy to get acquainted with her body, but short enough for him to still need to learn. Took me six weeks before I was able to keep from prematurely ejaculating around you, Bunny."

"Excuse me? I recall you doing that an all of two times."

"You didn't know about the others because I came before sex was even on the table."

"Ugh, Ken."

"Yes, Wife?"

She shook her head. "He better bang her soon. I want you to finger me."

His hand went from her knee to her inner thigh beneath her skirt. "I could do that anyway."

"The *bet*, though."

The bet Lana was about to win, for the Dom's sub followed a very specific order: don't cry out through three spanks. She persevered, and the man decided to reward her with nothing short of his cock thrusting between her legs.

Ken, having lost their loose bet, slipped his hand between his wife's thighs and stroked the length of her silk underwear.

"Oh, Kenny," Lana mumbled, leaning back in the couch so her husband could nibble on her lips. "You always knew how to please a girl."

His thumb pushed aside the thin material of her underwear and pressed into her wet folds. Lana began to slightly writhe, hand gripping his shoulder and legs opening in her skirt. "

"You're just easy, Bunny."

"Easy, huh?" Her breath stopped in her chest as the sub on stage shrieked in ecstasy, her Dom driving into her, hard, the audience sitting close enough to get a great view of the stage cheering their support. "You have to watch out using words like those. You might sully a woman's reputation."

"Oh, Lana..." One finger managed to push into her. "I made an honest woman out of you. Now you have to take it."

As she gasped, Lana caught sight of a woman sitting by herself nearby, watching them. *What a pretty young woman.* Petite. Curvy. Wearing a cream-colored piece of lingerie with matching collar. The girl was not attached to anyone, let alone a Dom, but she was probably looking for one.

You want some of this, girl? Lana opened her legs wider, exposing her husband's finger sliding in and out of her. *You can't have any. This man is all mine right now, and he's going to worship my pussy. Feel free to watch, though.*

Tingles shot through her toes as she watched this girl watch her. On stage, the solo sub could easily see some hardcore action, complete with wet skin slapping and eager little moans bouncing out of that girl's mouth. Yet instead she chose to watch Lana Andrews, an almost-forty woman, spread her legs, show off her goods, and let a man fuck her with one – no, two now – fingers. Lana let a groan roll out of her chest as she pulled one of her nether lips aside with her fingers and fell deep into the trap of making exhibitionist love with her husband.

"Fuck me harder," she hissed at him, pleased to feel him instantly thrust into her, more depraved with every passing second. More than one person watched them. That only fed into Lana's need to have sex, and she didn't care with *whom*.

She had no idea when her exhibitionism took a hold of her. Lana always had a "bad" streak in her when it came to the more taboo sides of sex. *I was eighteen when I had sex in public for the first time.* And that really meant public! Her then-boyfriend couldn't keep his hands off her at a house party. When he suggested he take her right there in the hallway, Lana hadn't hesitated in saying yes. Next thing she knew, she was claimed in front of a whole fraternity – and all that mattered was the thrill it gave her.

People loved sex. They loved watching others have sex. They loved thinking about sex, having sex, anticipating sex. There was a reason voyeurism was so prevalent to certain degrees. Lana was a betting woman, and she was willing to bet that many of those same voyeurs harbored fantasies of exhibitionism as well. Yet what most people didn't know was that you didn't have to be hot to get some in public. All you had to be was ready and eager. The happy watchers came on their own.

That's why God blessed the good green Earth with clubs like The Dark Hour. So kinky fetishists like Lana Andrews could get fingered by her husband in front of their corner of the room.

The fact that some people would rather watch her than the show on stage made her feel even hotter. She thrust her hips against her husband's fingers, taking them into her and feeling everything become even tighter. Ken groaned in her ear. Lana hooked her hand around the top of his tie and pulled, bringing him closer so he could kiss her throat.

You wish that this man were your husband. See how he works me? The perk to having one of the tightest cunts around was that anyone watching would think Ken's two modest fingers were the ticket to paradise. The way Lana clenched around them felt heavenly, as if her pussy had craved nothing more than these two specific fingers sent straight from the angels above.

Of course, it took more than a couple of digits to make her come so hard that her G-spot quivered in delight. It took a man who knew her body so intimately that he knew exactly how to stroke her, at what angle, and what to do with his mouth and words while he fucked his wife into another plane of existence. And, of course, any man who was going to give a woman a G-spot orgasm of her life did well to remember that it existed in the first place. And Ken never forgot. It helped that, for all of Lana's biological hang-ups downstairs, she was blessed with an easy to reach G-spot.

"That's it, baby," Ken growled into her ear. His fingertips took her, over and over, filling her, reaching deep within her, and stroking the most intimate parts of her body that she had ever shared with anyone. "Come for me right here."

Lana squeezed his tie and closed her eyes. She could feel the eyes of others on her, fueling her desire to perform for them. Bucking hips, rolling thighs, curling feet, and a mouth that wouldn't close because she was too busy thinking about coming to think of how she looked.

Fuck!

Sometimes, orgasm turned a woman like Lana Andrews into a wild, uncaged creature who couldn't be controlled by the best handler in the universe. This happened that night, when her husband drew a hard, unforgettable orgasm out of her. It zipped, no, *tore* through her, leaving no mercy in its wake as it tightened her abdomen and pussy both. "Ken!" she cried, nearly strangling him with his tie. "*Ken!*"

She felt more eyes on her. People who were summoned by her pealing voice and her plea for him to fuck her until she couldn't take it anymore. The show was long over on stage – the Dom came hauled his sub off the stage, so people needed *someone* to watch.

And why not watch me, the biggest star in this room? Lana reveled in that as she flung her head back on the couch and bucked her hips against her husband's fingers, each one three knuckles deep.

"My beautiful wife," Ken purred, Lana coming down from her ecstatic high. "Everyone else thinks you're beautiful too."

Damn, he always knew exactly what to say.

"Now give me these back, Bunny." Ken shook his fingers inside her, showing her how tight it was around them. "I need them, and you're about to snap them off."

She laughed, exhausted. "You would deserve it. I want to keep them inside me forever."

"My fingers, but not my cock?"

"There is a lot to say about a man's fingers, Kenny."

"They don't come, though."

Typical man, always thinking about the cum-shot. "Even so, I don't think I would mind hanging on to these for a while."

Nevertheless, Lana attempted to relax, releasing her hold on Ken's hand and letting him have all five fingers back. He gave her a mild punishment by inserting the wettest finger into her mouth, letting her suck it until she could no longer taste herself on him.

Meanwhile, she left her legs spread open. Who knew? Maybe someone liked what they saw.

"Have I called you beautiful yet today?"

"Yes, baby."

Ken wrapped an arm around her midsection, letting his wet fingers linger on her silky blouse. "I'll keep calling you beautiful until you're not anymore. But not only do I think that's impossible, but I would lie anyway. You deserve to feel beautiful every day of your life, Lana."

He sounded so sweet that Lana allowed herself to turn into a puddle of mush.

"You sweet talker." She sounded drunk. She *felt* drunk. Between the sex and the audience, Lana was liable to pass out on the couch for the rest of the night. Now, if only she were allowed to actually *do* that… "I need to go wash up." Lana found the strength within her to stand, pull down her skirt, and walk away from her dirty husband. He watched her head toward the women's restroom with a look that said she was more than welcome to finish him off when she got back. *I might.* Lana would prefer some actual intercourse in a private room, but she wasn't above giving her husband head before they headed home and had round two in their own room.

She found Elle standing in front of the bathroom mirror, sprucing up her makeup. "My favorite person," she chirped. "You're positively glowing. Let me guess. He went down on you during that show?"

"Close." Lana joined her friend at the sink and washed her hands. "Pussy pounding from the brother of the finger wearing his wedding band. And the middle one, I suppose."

"Good shit. Sorry I missed it."

Lana dried off her hands and leaned against the counter. "Still time for you to join us. My husband could use some disciplining, and I'm a bit worn out right now." Lana grinned. "How about you spank his naughty ass and I jerk him off. He'll love that."

Elle rolled her eyes. "Thanks. But I found me a date out there. I plan on spanking some other man's ass tonight. Tell your husband I send my sincerest apologies."

"Oh? Anyone I know?"

"Honestly?" Elle stood up straight, finished with her touch ups. "Probably. Is there any regular here you don't know?"

"Not really. Even if I don't like the person, I've probably learned everything there is to know about them. Or fucked them."

"You're crazy. I can't imagine screwing as many people as you have after saying wedding vows."

"Honey, that shit was *written* into our vows. My mother nearly had a heart attack."

"I bet she did." Grinning, Elle headed toward the restroom door and offered to open it for her friend. "Go take care of your husband's blue balls. I've got some of my own to tend to. Heh, not my *own*…"

"Uh huh." The moment Elle disappeared back into the club, Lana picked a bathroom stall and finished cleaning up.

She returned to the club expecting to find her husband talking to someone, since the man gabbed more than any woman Lana knew. She just wasn't expecting the exact person she found sitting on the couch with Ken, in the very spot Lana occupied only a few minutes ago.

It was the pretty, nubile sub who initially caught Lana's eye when she was being fucked for their corner of the club to see. There she was, looking cozy with Ken, who put a flirtatious hand on her shoulder and whispered something into her ear that made her giggle.

Flashes of Chloe the trampy maid took over Lana's mind. If her husband were fooling around with that girl, then this was probably what they looked like getting all cozy in his office. Probably one of the guest rooms. Her room. Who cared.

"Ah, Lana," Ken said the moment he noticed his wife standing before them. "Meet our new friend, Josie."

"*Our* new friend?"

The sweet brunette smiled meekly. "Nice to meet you, ma'am. I... really liked that..." She turned away, giggling.

She was the type of girl Lana would normally love to Top in front of her husband, but they had just enjoyed a threesome with their mistress that past weekend, and sometimes Lana thought she only had one threesome a week in her.

"Can I talk to you, Kenneth?"

His smile wavered, but his demeanor did not. "Of course, my love." He stood, sending a trite apology in Josie's direction. Ken followed his wife into a dark corner where they could be alone enough to convene on whatever was troubling her.

Everything was troubling her.

"I don't feel like fooling around with other people tonight. Get rid of her."

Ken was visibly taken aback. Whether at this being her reaction, or the force of it... "Sorry, Bunny, I thought you might like her."

"Like her? What is there to like about a weak little girl who can't hold her own against a virile woman like me?" Lana scoffed. "If you're going shopping for a woman for us, at least pick one who is more like me. I can't stand little muffins in my bed. That's more your bag, isn't it?"

The perplexity on Ken's face unnerved Lana. Could he not see what was going on? Did he not know that he was being so transparent? "Excuse me?" he said. "What's gotten into you?"

"Besides you tonight?" The huff wracking Lana's body was almost as strong as her orgasm from earlier. "It's not becoming of a man your age to flirt with twenty-year-olds who look like they came from a sub's nursery. It's creepy, Kenneth. Even our mistress at least acts like a grown woman for her age."

"Because she *is* a grown woman, Lana."

Words, words.

"And I don't appreciate you insinuating that about me." Ah, there it was. The hidden impatience of Kenneth Andrews. Sometimes Lana was able to get it out. And this was a man who had seemingly endless patience for her insecurities and crazy ideas. "You know damn well that I am not... like that." Like what, exactly? Why wouldn't he say it? "I thought she was attractive, regardless of how she chose to present herself. Yes, she's young, but she caught my eye, and I know you like taking control of more innocent women, and I thought… well, excuse me for trying to liven up the night a bit."

This was the moment Lana should have leaned into his embrace, kissed his cheek, and apologized. But she was not the type of woman to have those types of moments. She put her hands on her hips and shook her head instead. "Forget it, Ken. You know what? I want to go home."

"Already?"

"You heard me."

It was petty, but Lana was the queen of petty as of late. *Like I'm going to stand around and watch my husband flirt with a Chloe stand-in.* She realized what she was thinking, had a moment of panic, and immediately made the decision to call her therapist in the morning. She needed it.

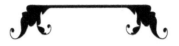

Chapter 7

"Everything's Fine."

"But you have no evidence that your husband is cheating."

There was that annoying word again. *Evidence.* Lana rolled over on her therapist's couch, wondering who he bought it from. *It's comfortable. I want it.* She wanted a lot of things.

"Does evidence really matter when my gut tells me something is wrong?"

"Perhaps something is, in fact, wrong or amiss." Her therapist was an elderly gentleman who was rumored to have single-handedly solved the Clintons' marriage. What he was doing in this God forsaken city of the rich and powerful, Lana had no idea. *Sucking my money dry, that's what.* The man charged thousands an hour. Not even "rich" people could afford him. *He better fix me.* If he could do it without pills? Even better.

Lana had watched pills destroy her mother's personality until she was nothing but a vapid shell who nodded politely and then went back to her jigsaw puzzles while guzzling orange soda – at least she wasn't drinking alcohol with the pills. *I'd rather die than become her.* Sister Inid was already on that path with her shitty husband and brood of kids.

The therapist cleared his throat before continuing.

"That doesn't mean he's cheating on you. All you've mentioned is a suspicious young maid mooning over your husband's stationery. Otherwise, isn't everything as it should be? No other problems? Money? Business? Your own personal sex life?"

"Everything's fine." They were rich. Business was always good. And sex? When were they not copulating like rabbits? *The other night notwithstanding.* Unfortunately, Lana still had a chip on her shoulder after they got home from The Dark Hour. Ken tried seducing her before they went to bed, but she shrugged him off, sending him to jack off in the bathroom. *I wouldn't even blow him.* That was a big deal for them. "Perhaps that's the problem. Everything is too fine."

"You're used to a certain level of chaos, aren't you?"

"I don't know if I would say that, but…" Lana chewed on the inside of her cheek, wishing she had some gum, a mint, anything to keep her tongue and teeth preoccupied with other than talking. "Things always change, eventually. Something always gives."

This was a truth in life. Or at least in hers. Nothing stayed nice and quiet forever. At some point, some business deal would flat line, somebody would go broke, someone would divorce, or, in her mother's case, someone would have a nervous breakdown and get doped up on Xanax and its ilk.

People died. Marriages ended. Children were born and created strained relationships for others. Houses were sold. In comparison to other people they knew, Lana and Ken were too quiet, wild sex life aside. They almost never disagreed regarding money and business, and if they did, it was sorted out rationally within a few days. When it came to sex, they were always on the same page, even if tastes changed here or there. *But at our core, it's business as usual.* It was always business.

"Ten years is a long time to be with someone," the therapist said. "Perhaps you are antsy?"

"I would believe that if we didn't have the kind of relationship we did."

"Do you still love him?"

"Of course I do!" What kind of question was that? Would she be here trying to sort out her insecurities if she didn't love the bastard? "Do I really have to spell that out?"

"I merely wanted to confirm, Lana." The man was more patient than Ken. Especially with someone as high-strung as Lana could be. "Do you believe he still loves you?"

"He says he does every day." How many women could say that after a decade of marriage? Only a lucky few, in Lana's experience. "He doesn't treat me any differently. We have a lot of sex. Three, four times a week. Sometimes more. Less if we're apart or sick, but that doesn't happen often." She glanced at her therapist. "I'm including non-penetrative sex with that." Oral and manual sex always counted in Lana's book. Otherwise she would've lost her virginity at sixteen and not fifteen, and she did love numbers with a multiple of five.

"All right." The therapist typed something on his tablet. "Now, Lana, I want to ask you something that may make you a bit defensive…"

She waited.

"Do you think it's possible that you are manufacturing this illicit affair between your maid and your husband?"

Lana turned toward him again. "Why would I do *that?*"

"Well, from the sounds of it, you're uncomfortable with how seemingly simple your relationship is after all this time. If your instincts tell you that things fall apart after a certain amount of time, then you will start looking for signs that may not even be there. Things that did not bother you before suddenly will now. You're looking for reasons to think that your husband is cheating, because you're looking for reasons to end your marriage. You said so yourself that you fantasize about divorcing your husband."

"I don't know if I would say *fantasize…*"

"It's completely normal, Lana. You are far from the first woman, let alone person, who harbors ideas of ending something perfectly fine for the sake of ending it. In this day and age, we are conditioned to want something new every five minutes. Even if you have an open marriage with your husband, you may still crave for someone new to call your own."

"I would never cheat on my husband."

A Fragile Wife

"Even so, our subconscious can sabotage even the best of things because of what it believes is necessary. And for your subconscious, it may think that a new relationship, a new marriage is in order. Therefore, you want a divorce, but you also need a reason for that divorce. You look for signs that your husband is cheating on you, one of the only reasonable grounds for divorce you can think of."

Lana sat up and swung her legs over the side of the couch. Her fingers gripped the edge as she stared at the plush, beige carpet. So neutral. So boring. Like her life could be sometimes, even for all its adventure. "So what do I do?"

"Well, first of all, you need to talk to your husband and tell him your fears and concerns."

Lana shook her head. "I couldn't tell him that I thought he was cheating on me…"

"You don't have to. Simply tell him that you're concerned about feeling uninspired and in need of something different. Whatever that means for you two. It may be necessary to brainstorm ideas on how you can eventually feel better and more confident in your marriage." The therapist paused, glancing at his ceiling in thought. "Your second honeymoon is coming up?"

"Yes. After our anniversary."

"That's an excellent opportunity to explore new facets of your relationship. It's also a chance to have these talks, since ten years marks a change in your relationship, no matter what."

She didn't want to cry. She definitely didn't want to cry in front of her therapist, whose office was decked out for

Christmas and sporting pictures of his happy family. Did this man have the same concerns for his life that she did for hers? Was he the type of man to build up signs that weren't there, so he would have the excuse of ending a perfectly good marriage? *I don't want to lose Ken...* And yet her instincts...

Lana grabbed a tissue and dabbed the corner of her eye. "I can't ignore my instincts. They've never failed me before."

"Then you really need to talk with him. If necessary, we can schedule a session with him."

Boy, that would be a trip and a half. Lana couldn't even imagine what that kind of conversation would be like.

She did leave the office that day with a new resolution, however. *Don't fall for your own mind games, Lana.* First, she treated herself to that spa day since she happened to be downtown. Lana was pampered by the best masseuse in the region and had her toenails painted a bright, cheery pink that would delight her every time she looked at them. She wasn't thrilled about having half her hair ripped out of her body, but she ignored the pain by talking to the esthetician about the latest gossip around town.

Lana considered these temporary improvements to her skin, nails, and muscles as a new lease on her attitude. *From now on, I'll calm down.* She strolled down the chilly city streets sipping a latte and trying to enjoy the moment for what it was.

Her husband loved her.

She loved her husband.

They had everything they could ever want, including each other.

Lots of people may not care much for them, for whatever reason, but those same people were jealous of how strong they were as a couple.

Lana could not let anything come between her and Ken, including her irrational insecurities conjured by her pesky subconscious. Her therapist was right. She was manufacturing these ideas for the sake of drama. No wonder some people found her insufferable.

She detoured to the downtown office where Ken was working that day. In true real estate mogul fashion, the Andrews owned their own renovated building that they used for their business and to sublet to others. Yet the top few floors were all theirs, and within those currently empty halls was her husband's downtown abode where he spent way too many hours a week dealing with grumpy investors, running numbers, and responding to concerns posted by current tenants and those looking to buy and sell other properties. All in a day's work for those two.

"Yes, thank you." Ken's voice echoed through the inner chambers of the private office the moment Lana entered. She quietly closed the door and tiptoed toward the sound of her husband's voice, intending to surprise him. "I love how willing you are, Chloe."

Lana stopped. So did her heart.

Color? What color? She didn't need any color in her face.

Ken wasn't talking to the maid back home like an employer. He leaned back in his large leather chair, knee resting against the desk as he spun himself to and fro with the dumbest

smile on his even dumber face. *Fuck me. Fuck him!* That voice…
that was the voice he used when talking sweet to Lana. To his
wife.

"*When I think of you, Bunny, I can't help but sound like this.*"
That's what he told her years ago, when she first asked him why
he spoke so softly like that. She had never heard it from any
other man, and she had yet to hear him talk that way to another
woman. Until now.

She was going to kill him.

"That's fine. Go ahead and put it on my desk. I'll put it all
away later." Laughter. "I've gotta go. I'll talk to you about it
later." Ken leaned forward, bending his elbows on his desk.
That stupid smirk would not leave his face. "I'll see you soon."

He hung up.

Lana remained in the archway, undetected. She stared at her
husband, the man who supposedly loved her above all others.
The man she took a vow to always be open and trusting with.
The man who was *definitely cheating on her.*

The therapist was wrong. So. Fucking. Wrong.

It wasn't all in Lana's head.

It was right here in front of her, and its name was a tale as
old as time. *My husband is screwing the help.*

Maybe not just screwing.

Romancing.

That was one boundary they never crossed: romancing
other partners. They would seduce, but they would never make
it emotional. That route led to nothing but tears and terror.

A Fragile Wife

Like now, as Lana faced her crumbling marriage before her very eyes.

"Kenneth."

She was going to do it. She was going to confront him.

He turned in his chair, surprised, but not shocked. The man had no shame! Here he was, getting off the phone with the *real* mistress while the wife walked in and caught him practically red-handed. If she didn't kill him, his lack of shame would.

"Bunny," he said, using that same voice he used with Chloe over the phone. "I wasn't expecting you."

No shit.

"Thought I'd drop by," she replied, tight-lipped. "Was in the neighborhood." *Asshole.*

Even though Lana stood in front of him like she was about to rip off his balls, Ken remained completely unfazed. How dare he be so composed? Didn't he realize what his wife had witnessed? "It's always a pleasure to see you, Wife. Did you drive down? We could go get dinner later. I hear there's a nice new Italian place a few blocks from here…"

Lana was going to cut straight to the point. "I heard you on the phone with the maid." She paused for emphasis. "Anything wrong back home?" *Like your dick in the wrong woman?* Lana heard that happened totally on accident sometimes.

"Oh? That?" Here it came. The lies. "Nothing of any concern. Chloe called me to inform me that a package I've been anxiously expecting arrived. I told her to leave it in my office to look at later."

Cynthia Dane

"Hey, baby, let's check out my package together... in my office." Gag.

"You sounded awfully familiar with her, Kenneth."

She continued to stand like an anxious soldier waiting for her orders. *Kill. Those are my orders.* Hell hath no fury…

"Why shouldn't I have been familiar with her? She's been working for us for months now." Finally, that man frowned. "What is this about? I'm telling you the truth, Bunny."

Lana lowered her arms, nearly letting her purse fall off her shoulder. *I want to believe him.* Why wouldn't she? She just came out of therapy, declaring how much she loved her husband and how much she wanted to believe that everything she'd been imagining was a lie. "Kenny…"

"Come here." Ken patted his lap.

She wanted to go. She wanted to flee – to go back to her therapist's office with this brand new information. *But I want him.* Lana took one tentative step forward, afraid that she would fall for her husband's demeanor once again.

This man wouldn't *really* cheat on her, right? It was all in her head, right? What was Lana to do? Did she trust her gut, which sent up a million red flags? Or did she trust her heart, that didn't care what her husband did as long as he treated her as he always did?

Your gut, stupid. What did her heart know? It made her go and sit in his lap, laughing away her worries because *how dare she?* Her heart was stupid. Couldn't she see that her husband going behind her back and romancing some young, insignificant woman *was* treating her like shit? Even if inadvertently?

It was days like those that not only caused a war within her body, but also proved how sad, stupid, and careless this drama queen really could be.

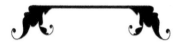

Chapter 8

"Does Lana Know About It?"

Christmas at the Losers Estate really was just that.

"*Low-siers*," Inid said to her youngest daughter. "It's not pronounced like that word!"

No matter how much she tried it, Inid would never be able to escape her maiden name. Like Lana, she had changed it the moment she married years ago. Inid Rothberg, however, never anticipated having to explain such a maiden name to her small children years after the fact.

"Still sounds like Loser to me..." said Collette, the youngest Rothberg child. "Why would someone call themselves that so long ago?"

"Times change, dear. It didn't used to mean that. I think." Inid patted her daughter's head and herded her toward the dining room. "We've got dinner, Collie. Now be nice for your grandmother."

"I don't wanna. She smells like gross."

Lana tuned them out. She didn't need to agree with her niece any more than she did. *Mother does smell like "gross."* Which happened to be how Lana felt most of the time now.

At first she blamed her period, which was unusually rough – probably compounded by stress, not that she could do anything about that at this time of year. Except then she worried there was something terribly wrong with her, so she went straight to her doctor two days before they left for the Christmas holidays. When he gave her the okay to travel, insisting that she was only "fretting," Lana nearly threw the biggest fit she ever threw in the doctor's office.

Ken was an utter gentleman through the whole ordeal. Including now, as he stood behind her at the dining room table, massaging her shoulders while talking to his older brother. At night he would massage her back, taking extra care of her abdomen until the terrible cramps finally abated long enough for her to sleep. He snuggled her. He kissed her. He never asked for the sexual things he sometimes did when they went without for a few days. He was a model husband, and that worried Lana.

Is he being nice because he's nice? Or is he being nice because he knows he's doing something bad? How deep did Ken's morality go? Would he feel bad about cheating on his wife? Shit, if he felt *bad*, he wouldn't be cheating on her! Right?

Or maybe the man misunderstood the boundaries of their relationship. *Maybe* he thought it was okay to fuck the maid because of the way their marriage was set up. Except he would've mentioned something by now. Said something stupid, like, "Maid's got nice tits, right?"

I could also still be making it up. There was a reason Lana hadn't confronted her husband... yet. She didn't have the concrete evidence. Everything was conjecture. Damn good conjecture, but a pleasant conversation on the phone and hearsay from the chef didn't a confrontation make.

So Lana chose to plow through life as it came. Right now it meant tending to her family's Christmas celebrations.

Even though Lana and Ken were by far the richest and most successful members of the family by every definition – meaning it was their families forced together – Lana's parents had the most bedrooms to house everyone. So once a year they packed their bags and headed upstate for a few days, relegated to the nicest guest room, even above Ken's parents, because they were the golden children.

Everyone was there. Lana's parents and her sister. Inid brought her children and husband, all a very picturesque family whom everyone agreed took the best holiday photos. Then there was Ken's family. His parents were there, and his three brothers happily were as well. One older, two younger. All but the youngest had a wife and children. Altogether, nine children of varying ages had the run of the place. Lana was the only woman at these functions who had no children, and her mother never let her forget.

Except for tonight, because Juliet Losers was too fucked up on Xanax and cider to remember to give her daughter grief for not following her biological destiny. *Last time she told me it was my duty to breed because of how rich I was.* Who was that money going to go to? Hilarious, because Ken's brothers sucked up to him for the sole purpose of sending their youngest kids to apprentice under him one day. There were plenty of nieces and nephews to pick from. Or maybe they would pick a kid off the street and change his or her life.

Lana thought these amusing things while she received her ongoing massage and fielded inane questions from her sister's husband. When Juliet made her appearance and sat at the head of the table next to her illustrious daughter, Lana decided that her niece was the smartest person in the family. Grandma definitely smelled like *gross.*

By the time dinner began, Ken sat next to his wife and began telling tales from the world of real estate. About half of them included his wife blowing up at some poor, hapless soul and busting his balls until he conceded to her demands.

Ken had an amazing way of making his wife sound like a total harpy, all while keeping a friendly smile on his face. Normally it didn't bother Lana – especially if it meant her reputation preceded her, and nobody would bother her – but tonight it only served as a reminder that even her husband saw her this way at times. What man wouldn't cheat on that?

She used to think that Ken wouldn't. Who knew...

The unfortunate thing was that she had no one to confide in. Not in her family, anyway. Usually these nights ended with her confiding to her husband about her feelings regarding her parents and sister. Ken was her best friend. *Ken* was her sound board and the man who reassured her that she was beautiful, smart, witty, and a tiger in the sack. Who knew how that would go tonight.

In truth, Lana didn't remember much about Christmas dinner. There was food. Kids whined. Brothers-in-law laughed and sisters huffed. Mothers popped Xanax. The in-laws insinuated that they wanted to go to Brazil for their upcoming anniversary, something that usually translated to a plea for money. Lana ignored it. If Ken wanted to give his money to his parents, so be it.

"Lana."

She snapped off auto-pilot sometime after dinner, when her husband leaned in and pointed to a maid carrying platters of pie. "Huh?"

"Pumpkin or blackberry, dear?"

"Oh. Pumpkin, please."

After dinner, Lana was obligated to spend time with her mother and sister in one of the studies. There she got to hear all about her brother-in-law's legal troubles at work. Something else she was expected to pitch in funds to help with.

"Perhaps if you want to save money, your husband should stop harassing his help."

Inid sniffed. "You know how men are. They chase tail. Be grateful you don't have kids. Ken wouldn't think twice about straying from you if he saw you as a mother."

"Inid," Juliet said sternly, the first thing she said in twenty minutes.

Lana pursed her lips. Her sister never stood a chance against her. "It's not kids that would do it, sweetie. It's the fact you haven't had a personality since you popped out the first."

"Lana!"

Maybe this was why Juliet Losers was on so much Xanax – raising these two assholes she called daughters. *At least one is filthy rich and the other gave her grandchildren.* That's all that mattered to a woman like her.

Lana didn't have a chance for peace until later that evening, when she excused herself to go to bed. The next day was Christmas, and although some in-laws would be scattering to see other family in the area, most of the brood would be at the Losers Estate to exchange presents. Lana wished she could remember what she got anyone…

"…She's going to lose her mind when she sees it." Ken's voice, in the library with his younger brother Travis. The two were always friends growing up, and things hadn't changed now. If Ken were to have a private conversation with anyone at a family gathering, it was *him.* "Chloe is already in love."

Lana stopped in the hallway. *Don't listen, idiot.* That's what her common sense said. Her gut? It made her stand outside that door, one ear completely open.

"Who's Chloe?"

"The maid. Man, listen for once. That's what I've been telling you this whole time."

"You sly ass dog.

Ken laughed."Don't I know it."

"Does Lana know about it?"

"Of course not. Would spoil everything."

"And this from the man who says the secret to a successful marriage is being open about and sharing everything."

"Trav, if I shared this with Lana, I may not *have* a successful marriage anymore."

"Good luck with that. I mean it. You're a crazy fucker, but good luck."

Lana moved on to the bedroom. *I see.* Ken was definitely keeping *something* from her. Something to do with Chloe. That if Lana found out about it? May mean the end of her marriage.

She was sitting on the edge of the bed when Ken arrived, all smiles as he said a chipper good evening to his wife and disappeared into the bathroom. When he reemerged a few minutes later, he had his hand clasped around a black box with a red ribbon.

"I know it's not quite Christmas yet," he said, sitting next to Lana on the bed. "But I wanted to give you this away from family eyes."

Detached from reality though she was, Lana took the box into her hands. *Jewelry.* The man had given her countless pieces of jewelry over the years. Earrings, necklaces, rings, bracelets... watches. Barrettes. Hairpins. Even a pair of nipple clamps. Yet she always counted on it being a carefully selected piece that her husband thought out well ahead of time. He never bought her something for the sake of buying it, or because he didn't know what else to get her. Like the finch pendant he gave her for her birthday. According to their mutual personal assistant, Lana's husband bought it two months before her birthday when he came across it in a store and thought of her.

The man has thought of me that recently…

"Thank you," she said graciously, pulling the ribbon off the box and popping the lid. "This is sweet of…"

She looked at a silver collar.

Then she looked at her husband.

"Go on. Take a closer look."

He said it so easily, as if it were no big deal for a man to buy his wife a sub collar for Christmas. Well, perhaps in their marriage it wasn't. For ten years they had been kinky to the max, after all.

Lana lifted the collar out of the box and inspected it. A simple, silver collar at first glance. Of course, the quality was superb. Nothing but pure silver, and a tiny chain for gentle tugging. This wasn't a collar to wear for serious play. It was the kind of collar for her to wear to The Dark Hour. The highlight, however, was the inscription on the inside.

"My Bunny."

Something swelled in Lana's heart. Or maybe it was in her gut.

"I know it's not much, darling," Why was Ken sounding so apologetic? Not every woman could say she got this kind of treatment ten years into her marriage. Most women were lucky if their men threw diamond earrings at them ten years in. "But I wanted to get you something special. For us."

He gently took the collar from her hands, unclasped it, and held it up to her neck. Lana pulled her hair aside and felt the snug collar enclose around her neck. "Thank you. It's lovely."

She knew what this meant. She doubted she was modeling her new present. Ken wouldn't have given it to her *tonight* if he didn't have something in mind.

"It looks good on you. How does it feel?"

"Fine."

"What's wrong?"

Damn him for being so intuitive. Briefly, Lana wished she had the kind of husband who didn't know his wife from being sick to healthy. Someone like Inid's no good husband. The bastard who also cheated on his wife. Seemed to be a running thread in life.

"I suppose I'm feeling a bit glum lately, Husband."

"Why is that?" His frown almost warmed her heart over. "Is it the... you know..."

Hilarious! They could talk about cum and saliva and God knew how many other body functions without flinching or blushing, but Kenneth Andrews still couldn't say "period" without tying his tongue in a knot. Men were hilarious when they weren't infuriating. "I suppose. I miss you."

"Miss me? Ah..."

He caught on quickly, especially since they had been sexually separated a lot longer than usual, but Lana knew he wasn't connected to the full story. And now was not the time to bring up her paranoia and suspicions.

Even now, her brain was churning in excuses. Reasons that she was being paranoid and there was no reason to worry about her sweet, friendly husband turning on her and fucking the maid behind her back.

And if he was…

How many other women had he seduced without Lana's presence or knowledge?

Sometimes it was more difficult than it was worth, being in the type of marriage she was. It was the only type of marriage she would accept, having the sexual appetite that she did. *A life without threesomes and swinging? Kill me.* Then there was the communication. That was the hardest part. Not communicating, but dealing with her partner's whims and own desires. It wasn't enough for Lana to say that she wanted to have a threesome with a man, and, oh, would her husband please suck the other man's cock for her amusement? No. Ken had to be in the mood, or at least open to the suggestion. He had to like the same man that his wife did, especially if he were the one doing most of the interaction. He had to like anyone they chose to play with. He had to understand where his wife was coming from. He had to have the energy and wherewithal to say, "Yes, Bunny, let's gang up on some lucky guy. Or girl. It doesn't matter."

Lana often told him stories about the years before they met. Her high school years. Her college years. Those glorious years of her mid-20s when she fucked any man who moved enough to satisfy her. Ken was not only the first man to keep up with her, but the first man to openly embrace the type of lifestyle and marriage she wanted. *I want a partnership. I want a husband. I want someone I can be a terror team with.* Someone she could always count on. Someone to always be by her side, even if other people came and went, as they always did.

They didn't have long-term girlfriends or boyfriends on the side, and the mistress didn't count. She was an amusement for them both to enjoy. No, what Lana meant was a truly polyamorous relationship, not swinging. Ken never asked about getting a girlfriend, and Lana was never interested in being serious with another man. Until now, it wasn't even something she considered. Why would she *want* another man like that when she had her husband to fulfill all those needs? It sounded bothersome.

When Ken kissed her that Christmas Eve night, Lana felt both relieved and apprehensive. A part of her desperately wanted to make love. Slow, gentle love that would open her heart and reassure every part of her that worried… and that was a lot of parts.

Yet Ken wasn't in the mood for slow, gentle love. His wife could tell that from the way he gripped her arms, possessively, his heavy kisses pushing her back toward the bed and overtaking her lithe frame. Yeah, he was about as in the mood for slow and sensual sex as Lana was in the mood to find out he was cheating on her.

Her husband being hungry enough to devour her should have been riveting. And yet here Lana Andrews was, wishing she wasn't… as enthralled with the idea as he was.

"I missed you too," he said into her ear, his breath so heavy that she almost shuddered to feel it. "I hope you're feeling well enough to let me in tonight."

Let me in. They had many code words. Such words were necessary in the public sphere, where they loved to incessantly flirt and make plans for kinky times later on. In front of people who would be appalled to know it, no less. *Let me in* not only meant fucking her, but in the sort of way that most frequenters to The Dark Hour would be excited to watch.

"Kenny," she said. "We can't. This is my mother's house. There are children down the hall."

"So? You think I haven't thought of that?" Ken chuckled, his hand going up her abdomen and brushing against her breasts. *Damn you both for responding to him so readily.* "I already knew I was going to ask you to be... shall we say... silent?"

Shivers went down Lana's spine. Ah, her husband posed a challenge. The type of challenge she would normally jump in joy to take on. *"Be as quiet as a mouse, Bunny. I only want to hear whimpers and little moans come from those pouty lips. That's your goal... fulfill that, and I will give you the orgasm of your life."*

Usually Lana Andrews enjoyed the possibility of being caught mid-coitus with her husband. Locked up in her parents' house with a bunch of relatives around was one of the few times she *didn't* want that.

"You ask a lot of me right now, baby."

"I thought you might like it, actually. You've been so down recently, between holiday stress, work, and your illness. I'll do all the work." Ken flicked the tiny chain leash hanging from her new collar. "I know you like asserting yourself most of the time, but I think it's good for you to relax once in a while and let your husband take care of you…"

"Take care of me?" Lana had to laugh at that. "The way you're talking right now, Kenneth, I know you're not thinking of anything slow. You want to fuck my damned brains out."

"Bunny, you know me too well.' Ken sucked the bottom of her earlobe, his fingers circling one of her nipples through her sweater. *Damn it for feeling good.* Even if she weren't paranoid about her marriage, would she be in the mood for this? *Probably.* Damn it! "Is it so bad for a man to want to completely dominate his beautiful wife? I guess I've missed you so much that all I can think about is taking you to the point you want to scream… but can't."

"You've thought about this."

"Yes."

A lot of people had the wrong impression about their dynamic. Those looking at them from the outside tended to assume that Lana was the dominant one in the relationship, even when she was being dominated *by* her husband. As if she were some total power bottom getting her way. In truth, Lana truly loved being dominated, especially by Ken. It was a facet of their relationship, but a powerful one. Sometimes all Lana could think about was her husband putting her "in her place," providing domestic discipline, and spanking her until she was pink and raw.

She wasn't sure that tonight was one of those nights.

"I love you, Bunny."

He said it so sweetly that she nearly melted. *Be careful, Lana. Your heart.*

It was that blasted heart that sent her straight to Ken's arms. It was that neglected body that succumbed to whatever he wanted to do. No, it was her mind that was the most vulnerable. Her mind knew what a bad idea it was, but it held no power in this situation. She was Ken's, body, heart, and soul. He would never possess her mind, and normally that was okay. Lana could reconcile that. Yet tonight, as her husband stuffed her mouth with one of his silk ties and bound her to the headboard, Lana cursed her ability to separate her mind from the rest of her. Everything else inside her could go along with Ken's plans for her. She could feel love. Aroused. Fulfilled. So why couldn't she let her subconscious in on all the fun?

Because deep down, I know. She probably wasn't the only woman Ken tied up, gagged, and fucked until she was begging for orgasm. There may be other women out there he claimed to love as much. Maybe he told them he was planning on divorcing her and marrying them. Were those girls dumb enough to believe it? How dare they! They would never be as good as Lana Losers, the original Mrs. Andrews.

I really am a loser, though. That thought cut short her climax, but not her husband's. He came long, hard, and deep within her, his hot breath slamming against her chest as he stilled within her and unleashed himself.

Usually Lana found that moment the hottest. Her husband, a usually composed man, unable to control himself to the point his biological impulse took over and attempted to... well, did it really have to be said? *We've role-played impregnation a few times…* Lana wasn't interested in becoming a mother, but damn if it wasn't hot to hear her husband, her Master, whisper, "I'm gonna own your body," just moments before his orgasm.

The reason that sort of thing turned her on was because, until now, Lana believed that she was the only woman her husband "owned." No matter who else they played with, how many women they took on, Lana would always be Ken's one and only when it came down to it. She didn't hesitate to believe that, if her husband had to choose one woman for the rest of his life, it would be her. Wasn't that what he declared when he married her ten years ago?

"Merry Christmas," Ken said, long after he untied her and removed her brand new collar from her throat. He kissed her cheek and wrapped his arm around her as the lights went down and he fell into an undisturbed sleep.

Lana had to get up and head to the bathroom. She watched Ken roll over and continue sleeping, her feet taking her to the sink in the adjacent room.

She stood in front of the mirror, her naked body more pathetic than usual. She saw every crease, every wrinkle of age. The lines she worked so hard to keep at bay. What she once thought was vanity she now believed was *fear*.

Fear that she would get too old. That she would go from being Ken's wife to his stand-in mother. The more she looked at herself in the mirror, the more she realized her body was closer to forty than she ever anticipated.

Lana whipped her arm across the counter and knocked her husband's shaving cream and razor onto the floor.

I need help. Her fingers gripped the edge of the sink, blond hair cascading against porcelain. *I'm gonna lose it at this point.*

She had two options: keep staying the course, wondering if her husband was cheating her on, or tackle the issue head on.

She may regret it. She may make a total fool of herself if her instincts were wrong. But Lana Andrews could not continue to live with the constant worry and misery that her husband was anything less than the wonderful man she always thought he was.

Ten years of marriage depended on it.

Chapter 9

"Stay Away From My Husband."

Lana was more than grateful to put the rigors of Christmas behind her. As soon as she and Ken returned home, she slept for a day, putting off all work in those pivotal few days between Christmas and New Year's. Her husband asked if she were ill again, and all she could say was that the weather – which was unusually wet and chilly that year – was dampening her spirits. He responded by closing the curtains, keeping a fire stoked in their room, and turning the flat screen hanging above the fireplace to every tropical travel show he could find. By their anniversary, on the 29th, Lana swore she would never go to the Caribbean again.

Ugh. Their anniversary.

A Fragile Wife

Due to her health, Lana could not join Ken for their reservations at their favorite restaurant in town. They also had to cancel their plans to occupy a honeymoon suite at the Presidential Hotel, something they had been planning all year – the equipment they had accumulated remained unboxed in the closet. The last thing Lana wanted to do was have kinky sex with her husband. Something he caught wind of fairly quickly, often asking her if she wanted to go to a doctor – any kind of doctor.

Her therapist was away for the holidays. Too bad. *I'm sure he would love to hear my recent paranoid ramblings.*

"Bunny," Ken said on their anniversary, sitting on her side of the bed and patting her hand. Lana turned off the TV to hear what he had to say. "What's wrong? You're worrying me."

She shrugged, as if how she felt meant nothing. *I don't want to talk about it right now.* She wanted to sleep, to play mindless games on her tablet, and to read all those literary classics she had yet to catch up on.

"Perhaps it's seasonal depression," she offered.

"You've never been this bad before."

How kind of him to notice over the years.

"You're not… *depressed* depressed, are you?"

Oh, Ken… he had such a way with words. Sometimes. Not all the time. "Maybe. I don't know, Kenny. There are things weighing me down right now." Tears formed at the corners of her eyes. "I'm sorry I ruined our big anniversary…"

"Don't do that. You haven't ruined a thing." He wiped away one tear, but missed the other one. "I don't care what we do, as long as we're together. Besides, we can make up for it on our honeymoon. Are you still looking forward to that?"

She nodded. *I had been, anyway.*

"You can tell me what's bothering you. When have you not been able to tell me anything?" Ken squeezed her hand, a touch she would usually welcome with everything she had. "You know I like knowing what's going on in that beautiful head of yours. Please, Lana, you're starting to scare me."

Scare him? *Scare* him? Lana was the one wasting away here. She was the one battling her subconscious in a game of wills she could not afford to lose. She had hoped to have the air cleared regarding her husband's fidelity by now, but her illness put her behind schedule to the point she refused to let Chloe into the master suite, citing that she didn't want to possibly spread anything. Either Roberta brought things directly to her or Ken took care of everything when he got home. He didn't even complain when Lana was too sick to go to an important business meeting right after Christmas.

"Lana?"

She squeezed his hand back. "I'm worried that I'm seeing things that aren't there."

Her husband sat back with a start. "What do you mean by that? Do you mean like…?"

"I don't mean mental illness." She snorted. "Unless I really am depressed or anxious, I guess. I'm not turning into my mother." Another snort, this time of derision. "I mean I think my brain is fabricating situations that aren't really there, because it can't believe that happiness lasts this long."

A Fragile Wife

Although his face said he didn't understand a damn thing she said, the words coming out of Ken's mouth were completely different. "Bunny," he began. "Come downstairs. I have something I want to show you."

He helped her into her nicest silk robe and led her down the hall, down the stairs, and into the dining room, where an elaborate candlelight dinner was set. Lana sat down, shocked but unable to express it. Ken sat next to her, his hand never letting go of hers.

"Happy anniversary, Bunny. Here's to ten more."

Champagne, a delicious meal, and their mutual favorite of chocolate pecan pie. It overwhelmed Lana, who started sobbing halfway through their meal. Ken didn't say anything. He held her hand and cleaned up the carrot she had dropped with her fork. *I don't deserve this man.* Even if he were cheating on her, she didn't deserve him.

That was a dangerous thought.

***

Luckily, Lana was a woman who could get over herself as quickly as she fell into the trap of being *so into* herself.

By New Year's, she was better. Out of bed and back to work, at least. She and Ken attended a party at Le Château with most of the other patrons and a few of their guests. They were congratulated on their ten year anniversary and asked if they had any advice for the budding couples around them. Ken said it took "a lot of patience and communication."

Their love life returned to somewhat normal. Not as kinky, but at least Lana was in a place where she felt good enough letting her husband back into her body. Ken did not complain. It tired Lana having the model husband who only served to make her feel guiltier for her suspicions.

By the first week of January she was back downtown, attending meetings, busting balls, and having lunch dates with people beside her husband. If it weren't for the ghost haunting her brain, Lana would consider herself back to completely normal and business as usual.

Except things could never be left alone. Not when she and Chloe lived in the same damn house.

More than once she considered firing the girl, giving her a nice severance check and referral, and hiring a butler – not that it would stop anything. If Ken had been cheating on her, he would move on to someone else – including the butler. Her husband's tastes for men were nowhere near as strong as they were for women, but with Lana's paranoia cranked to the max, she trusted no one, man or woman. Her best bet was hiring an older maid who had the sex drive of a eunuch.

She saw her chance to tackle things, however, one sunny – but cold – day the second week of January. It was one week before she and Ken boarded their flight for their second honeymoon, and she was not going to let certain opportunities pass her by.

Especially when she found Chloe sitting on a bench during her break, flipping through more of Ken's personalized stationery.

"What is that?' Lana demanded, swiftly approaching the young maid before she could see the oncoming storm and put the evidence away. "What has my husband given you?"

Chloe gaped at her, caught red-handed. God, she looked barely a day over eighteen. In truth, she was in her early 20s, but had such a baby face that Lana wouldn't blame her husband for lusting after her. In another situation, Lana may lust after her as well. *We would both devour you, girl.* Lana didn't want to consider the thought right now. Not with the *help*.

"It's nothing, ma'am. Just a list of instructions."

Bullshit. Chloe made a grave mistake not hiding those papers. Lana attempted to snatch them right out of the maid's hands... but Chloe's grip was so strong that the papers tore in half. All Lana had to show for her tantrum was the letterhead and the tops of words she could not make out in her husband's cursive writing.

"Look here," she growled, pointing a steel-tipped boot in Chloe's direction. "I know what's going on here. You're staying low for now, but a wife knows when hanky-panky is underfoot. My husband is an idiot who thinks he can get away with it. You?" Lana cackled. That same cackle that sent so many of her colleagues running and calling her "crazy bitch" behind her back. Or right in front of her. "You're nobody. I can wipe the floor with you. I can make sure nobody hires you in the city for as long as you live. Got it?"

At first, Chloe merely looked *petrified*. Now, Lana did not enjoy scaring a girl shitless. It wasn't as satisfying as, say, scaring a fellow CEO shitless. There was no joy, no pride in making some little no-name girl quake in her flats and act like she was going to relieve her bowels in front of the boss.

Chloe changed. Knowledge overcame her. Soon enough, she knew exactly what her crazy-ass boss was referring to.

"Oh my God!" she cried, crumpling the yellow stationery in her hands. "I swear I'm not... no... you have the wrong idea, Mrs. Andrews!"

"Do I? You think I haven't played this game before?" A part of her wished the change in Chloe's demeanor meant a tiger cub was about to burst out. Threatening, but nothing she couldn't deal with. Instead she got a scared little girl who probably really believed what she was saying. "You would be remiss, Chloe. I know exactly what my husband is up to."

"You... do?"

"Oh, yeah. And I know your role in it, if you know what I mean."

Now the maid looked confused.

"Mind yourself," Lana said as a final warning. "I wouldn't merely destroy you, girl. I would make your life such a living hell that you would have to move to the other side of the country to get a break from me. And even then? I would find you. Stay away from my husband."

"I..."

"Shut up." Lana turned, a satisfied grin taking over her pale complexion. "Oh, and I believe your break is now over. Roberta has some things for you to do."

Lana learned nothing from that encounter, but damn if she didn't feel better!

Chapter 10

"Do You Think I'm Pretty?"

"Oh, boy," Elle said over margaritas the next afternoon. "Bullying your maid? That's a new low, even for you."

Lana slammed her margarita on the table between them and squared her shoulders. "I did what had to be done. You think I liked doing that?"

"Yeah, I do. At least a little." Elle laughed, pushing out her fake tits and brushing her manicured nails through her crunchy black hair. *Outside of the club, you can really tell she does shit to herself.* Lana hoped she never reached that level of delusion. "You like throwing your weight around. Nothing wrong with that, especially from a badass bitch like you, but was it really necessary to make your *maid* piss herself? Even if you think your husband is hiding his sausage in her taco, that was brazen. Jesus, Lana."

Yup. I've told someone. When Elle called her up the night before, wondering if she wanted to do afternoon drinks downtown, Lana jumped on the chance. She needed someone to bounce her suspicions off. Elle was as good as it was going to get on short notice.

"I can't believe that *Ken* would cheat on you. Honey, that man is over the moon for you. Even after ten years, I can tell from the way he looks at you. You could tell him no more orgies for the rest of your lives, and he would go along with it as long as he got to be with you."

"See, that's what I've tried telling myself." Lana lined up their empty glasses before sitting back in her seat, arms crossed. "I know the man still loves me. But is he fawning over me to keep me placated and distracted, or is it all in my head?"

Elle shook hers. "You're a mess. Are you taking this attitude with you on your second honeymoon? That should be a time for mindlessly boning your husband until he ain't got a drop left in him. Don't take the mind games with you. If you don't have this all cleared up by the time you go, then you might as well not go at all. I'm serious."

"Says the woman who has never been married."

"Don't give me that! You know no man can keep me tied down. It's more like me keeping them tied up."

Lana ignored that. *She has a point, but I don't want to admit it.* Classic. "What do I do, though? I can't ask him if he's cheating on me."

"Obviously. But you need to do something before you destroy your marriage over something as stupid as thinking your husband is cheating on you – when he's not. I still don't believe it for a second. Normally I'll go along with a girl's suspicions, but Ken? *Ken?* This is the man who would erect a Taj Mahal for you should you die right now."

"Look, Elle, I'm not debating whether or not he loves me." Lana leaned against their table, the rabble of other patrons in their sunny café nearly drowning out her words. "The man could still be super in love with me but still keeping a side piece. You know how dumb men can be. Even Ken could fall victim to his second brain doing all the talking."

"Here I thought you had more respect for your husband."

"I don't wanna hear it."

"Hey, I'm a neutral party. I'm not gonna be Team Lana without any proof. You've got one woman's shifty account, your maid reading your husband's stationery, and their private conversations that sound suspiciously like flirting. I'm sorry for what you're feeling, Lana, but that's not enough. You need to either split or step up. *Before* you do something really dumb."

"You sound like me doing something 'dumb' is a given."

For some reason, Elle ignored that. "What are you two doing tonight? You wouldn't come into town solely to meet me. You two must be up to something this fine Friday night."

"We're having dinner and then going to The Dark Hour."

"Oh, fun. Wish I could join you, but I've got a business dinner that will last all night. Then I'm going to bed. I'm too old for the party life you and Ken still have."

"I'd hardly call it that."

"What are you doing at the club?"

Lana shrugged. "Not performing, if you're asking."

"Oh, it is." Elle chuckled. "If you were, I may have to cancel and ask that you two hold off until 10:30 for me to get my ass there to watch."

"Pervert."

"I do my best." Elle lowered her voice. "Going to that club could be your opportunity to *really* see how he feels about you. Confirm some suspicions or not. I mean, it depends on what you're up to doing."

"We'll see." Lana had to chuckle as well. "You know, it's been over a month since I last called my cousin the lawyer. You'd think I'd be blowing his phone up right now."

Elle cocked her head to the side. "Then that means deep down you think this marriage is worth saving. Even if you're saving it from yourself."

Sometimes Elle could be an ass, but she was usually right.

***

The club was unsurprisingly busy that Friday night. It was always busy Friday nights, much to Lana's delight.

People flirting. People fucking. People flirting and fucking at the same time. She knew she was with her kind when she stumbled upon a man getting a blowjob whilst trying to pick up another couple for some swinging fun later.

"Have we played with them before?" Ken asked, his hand wrapped around hers as they searched for a couch to sit on. "He looks familiar."

"Please, Kenneth." Lana put her free hand on his shoulder. "July. I blew him, you blew me…"

"Ah. Right. I barely recognize him because I spent most of that night staring at your pussy."

"As you should." *Mine above all else.* "If we're not careful, though, this club will start getting stale. Needs more fresh blood around our age." No fun playing with college kids who managed to find their way in there. The occasional single was fine, even fun, but couples were so far up their own asses that neither Lana nor Ken could fuck them if they wanted. *Rude. They're rude.*

"There's nothing wrong with repeat lovers, Lana."

They finally found a couch, recently vacated by a couple who were probably too frisky for people to deal with. They looked like they were headed to a private room, and it didn't take long for a club attendant to come by, clean up the glasses and beer bottles, and quickly wipe down the couch. *Delicious!*

"What do you want, Lana?" Ken was already ordering drinks before the attendant could get away from them. "Should I get your usual cosmo?"

"I'll have some wine, actually. I don't want anything hard."

After Ken ordered their drinks, he sank back into the couch and wrapped his arm around his wife's shoulders. "Never a dull night in this place, huh? I've seen four pairs of tits already."

You would be looking, huh? "Well, I've seen five cocks."

"Really? I only saw three."

Lana patted her husband's thigh. "This one doesn't count?"

"It's not hard yet, so no."

Lana could've done something about that, but decided to pull away and check out the sights. *A lot of action tonight.* Blowjobs, handjobs, nipple twisting, fingering, and enough making out to spread a mess of mononucleosis. Lana could smell the sweet scent of sex on the air, no matter how much perfume the club pumped into the house of sin. It was only a matter of time before everything was covered in bodily fluids.

The stage was rarely empty. From the moment they arrived, some Dom or Domme was giving some poor sub's ass a spanking or riding them like a proper pony. People shrieked, laughed, and purred in appreciation. The applause was endless, whether it was two women or a man and a woman on the stage. These were the types of nights Lana loved the most. She fed off the sexual energy, wishing to have a piece of everyone she came across – all the better if her husband watched. *The difference is that I wouldn't fuck anyone without him there.* She hoped her husband understood that distinction.

"What do you fancy tonight, my dear wife?" Ken asked, his hand slipping over Lana's knee. "Tonight's our last chance to have some fun with someone before going on vacation. Although who knows? Maybe some cabana boy or bikini girl will end up in our den of sex."

"You would like that, wouldn't you?" Lana nursed her wine, hoping the alcohol would kick in soon. "My husband is always looking out for my best interests. Like getting laid."

"You know, Bunny, I've been thinking..." His hand squeezed her knee so hard that she nearly flinched. "It's been a while since I saw you with..."

"Hmm?" She caught on, soon enough. "You really are a pervert. You're probably the only man even in this room who gets hard at the thought of his wife fucking another man."

"Have you never heard of cuckolding? Shocked. Although… it's not cuckolding if I'm 100% on board. Or at least I don't think it is."

Lana laughed. "Still, you're hard pressed to find a man around here who wants to pimp his wife out."

"Honey, the more you talk about that gangbang in college, the more I think I know what we're doing for your fortieth birthday."

See? This was the kind of banter and flirting Lana loved in her marriage. Only Ken would think about his wife fucking another man in front of him and get *hard*, not jealous. Then again, the man got hard thinking about fucking another woman in front of his wife. Lana didn't think these kinds of marriages were possible before Ken proposed to her ten years ago.

"That was a great night." Lana often thought of it fondly. Who said only bad experiences happened in frats? "Tell you what. You start garnering interest in gangbanging this hot body, and we'll talk. I'll only do hot guys."

Ken nodded to a young man sitting with another. "Like him?"

Lana snorted. "That's the smoothest chest I've ever seen. He's either gay or taken."

"Like all the good ones, right?" Her husband's breath was unexpected in her ear. "Like your good ol' husband."

Cynthia Dane

His hand traveled from knee to thigh, slowly opening his wife's legs and making her breath catch in her throat. "Indeed, Husband." She inhaled, deeply, controlling the lust and arousal burning within her stomach. "You're a man who isn't like others. You actually want to see your wife get fucked."

"By as many people as possible."

Lana blushed, hiding it behind her glass of red wine. "You know how difficult that can be for me…" Her legs crossed, over her husband's hand.

"That only makes it hotter." Ken cornered her in the couch, arms wrapped around her, legs coming for hers, his lips nibbling sweetly at her throat. The only thing keeping them apart was that glass of wine clenched tightly in Lana's hand. "Baby, you know what I want tonight."

Lana's throat went dry. Even if she drank that whole glass of wine in one gulp, her throat would still be dry. "I can guess." Her thighs clenched together.

In case he hadn't made his point clear yet, Ken went ahead and drove it home into Lana's brain. "I want to see you take on the biggest cock in the room."

She was trapped between arousal and freezing up so badly that nobody would be able to thaw her out that night. "Why?"

Ken loosened his hold on her, as if he couldn't believe she asked that. "Because it's hot."

"You think it's hot watching me hurt like that?"

"I…" Ken removed his arm from her shoulders. "I didn't know that's how you really felt about it. I thought you liked it once in a while."

A Fragile Wife

Lana put her wine down and held her forehead in her hand. She was lucky to wear such a tight up-do that day, otherwise she risked annoying herself with her own hair. "Well," she said, forcing a smile. "I certainly don't *hate* it once in a while."

She looked at the young man they spotted earlier. He was probably in his late 20s. A sub allergic to shirts and wearing pants so tight she could see what he packed around. *Nine inches, at least.* Unless he was a shower, not a grower. In which case that probably worked in Lana's favor.

Otherwise, he was the run of the mill male sub. His eyes met Lana's more than once, and she flashed him her most winning expression: Domme mixed with relentless vixen.

"Look at you," she put out into the world, *"Some posturing man who doesn't understand his only use is to please me."* She wrapped her hand around her husband's leg. *"Do you understand that this is my husband? I make love to this man all the damn time. He knows I'm looking at you. Do you know what that means? It means he wants a piece of you too. You have no idea who you would be dealing with."*

"You would be into watching me bang some frat boy with a bigger cock than brain." Lana glanced at her husband, reveling in his confusion. "You think I would go down easy? You would be wrong, Kenneth Andrews. I'd take that dick like a pro, small pussy or not."

"Maybe, just maybe…" Ken leaned against her, his weight almost imposing. "It's that 'or not' part I'm most interested in."

"You know, sometimes you still manage to surprise me."

"I could say the same to you, my sweet. Remember, you were the one who originally suggested this a long time ago."

"Of course I remember. Sometimes I'm stupid and think taking a huge cock is easy."

"I wouldn't say *stupid*. More like adventurous."

"Hmph." Lana clicked her tongue, but did not really feel like further admonishing her husband. "And what do you get out of it? Besides my humiliation."

"Humiliation? Please. Maybe I like the sheer look of surprise on your face when that kind of man first takes you."

Shivers went down Lana's spine. Whether they were sexual or not, she wasn't sure. "It doesn't bother you? I mean… having another man inside me like that. I'm your wife."

"I don't know what that has to do with it. You're your own sexual being. Surely, just having me can get a bit boring. It's not a bad thing for us to share this kind of thing."

"You're rarely boring, darling."

"Appreciated. Although I'm not sure why you're bringing this up now after so many years. You've been acting so strange lately."

Had she? About this? "It's not a bad idea to talk these things over once in a while. You know, check in and all that." Lana rubbed her husband's arm. "Tastes change. Our desires… well, they change too."

"What are you trying to say? That you're not into it anymore?"

Me? Hardly. "What I'm saying is that just because you were okay with some other man fucking me whenever we last did it, doesn't mean you're down with the idea now. I love you, Kenny. I want you to be happy with me."

A Fragile Wife

A part of her felt weak. Wimpy. Selfish. Here she was, practically throwing herself at her husband. Emotionally, anyway. Didn't he still love her? Didn't he want to do all the things they used to do? Didn't that fulfill him? *Please, please... tell me that we have enough thrills to keep you with me.* Lana couldn't handle finding out her husband was cheating because he needed that thrill of hiding something from his wife. It would destroy her.

"I am happy with you. I've been the happiest man on Earth these past twelve years." He kissed her cheek, motioning to the young man they both lusted after. "You're freaking me out a little, Bunny. I can only imagine what you have planned."

She didn't have anything planned, but he didn't have to know that.

"Stay here and let me work." Lana handed him her wine and stood up, letting her feet carry her across the room and to the young men surrounding a small table full of drinks. Her eyes remained on the masculine specimen who had an anaconda slithering up his tight pants. *Wish I had kept my drink.*

The man looked back at her, his laughter abruptly ending the moment he realized that Lana only had eyes for him.

"Scram," she told the other subs. "I saw the Domme posse come stalking in a few minutes ago. I'm sure some pussy awaits you there."

The other men glanced at each other before getting up. Although Lana was not *their* Domme tonight, she was definitely Domme enough to make them obey. And if she wanted them to leave her alone? They damn well would!

Left with the young man she had been eyeing for the past few minutes, Lana sat next to him, her body language inviting and words even more so.

"You seem like the type of man looking for a good time."

He sat up straight. He may be a sub, but he was still a man, and Lana was used to these younger types flexing their (nice, very nice) muscles even if they didn't realize it. *I was graduating high school when he was born, I would bet money on it.* All right, maybe middle school. Fifth grade pageant? Did it matter? *Not in these situations, it doesn't.*

"I am looking for whatever a good Mistress provides." The shirtless man reached forward, pouring Lana a small amount of craft beer in a clean glass. He offered it to Lana, who took it to be polite even though she wasn't a fan of beer.

"And what name do you offer a Mistress who comes your way?" Lana huffed. "Or do you prefer to have your Mistress give you a name for the night?"

"My name is Caden."

Oh my God, of course it is. Lana wanted to laugh. Half her nephews were some form of Aiden, Hayden, Trayden, God knew what else. They all blurred together for her. "Well, Caden, what if I told you that Mistress is looking for a man who can fulfill a specific function tonight?"

He raised his eyebrows. "I would say it depends on what that function is, ma'am."

Lana brushed back some of the dark hair growing on his forehead. Her touch had the desired effect: Caden flinched, muscles flexing and smooth skin warming to the touch.

"Let me ask you first, Caden... do you think I'm the type of woman you would follow?"

He looked her up and down, sizing her up. Not just her body. Most subs didn't care about that, although a good looking Mistress was a huge bonus. No, he was sizing up her strength, her willfulness, the way her eyes gazed at him seductively. He assessed her fingers as they gently rubbed the top of his hand. Her voice, calm but stern, spoke to those desires that weren't so hidden inside a man like Caden.

"Very much so, Mistress."

"Good. Because I like you too, Caden. You seem obedient. And you seem to have..." she glanced at his cock. "Talents."

"I aim to please, Mistress."

"Well, let me tell you what kind of thing I have planned tonight, *Caden.*" She gestured to her husband sitting a ways away. Ken gazed back at them, although he covertly checked his cell phone, crossed his legs, and finished his wife's wine for her. The right mix of interested and disinterested. "See that man there? That's my husband. We just celebrated our tenth anniversary."

"Congratulations, Mistress."

"I don't tell you this to make anyone jealous. I tell you this because my husband and I have been looking at you all night – if you couldn't tell."

"I may have noticed. I need to tell you, though... I'm not so interested in men. I'm sorry, Mistress."

"My husband doesn't feel touchy tonight. He has other plans for us. Plans that may involve you, if you're game."

"Oh?"

Lana pushed her lips toward his ear. The man wore enough aftershave to scare off any normal woman, but Lana had smelled so much cologne, perfume, and aftershave in her years that she couldn't be bothered with it any longer. *In our early days, Ken hadn't yet learned how to control his scents.* Some men needed a wife to do everything for them. Like teach them basic manners when it came to their fashion and hygiene choices.

"Yes," Lana whispered, ignoring that potent aftershave. Weaker women would have run. "My husband likes to watch sometimes. He likes the idea of a young, obedient man taking his wife he's had for over ten years. Do you know what that's called?"

"I think it's called cuckolding, ma'am."

"This isn't cuckolding. If a woman has ever used you to cuckold, then you know the surprise on a man's face when he finds out what his wife's up to. This is for everyone's mutual pleasure. You get me…" Lana wrapped her hand around Caden's thigh, coming dangerously close to his hardening cock. *Good thing he seems to like me.* "I get what you're packing around in these pants of yours, and my husband gets the extreme pleasure of watching it all happen. What do you think?"

Caden looked between her and Ken, assessing what they offered. "And there's no touching between me and him?"

"Of course not, especially if you're not into that." Now, if Caden *were* into that, Ken would probably do more than watch in the beginning. "Why don't you come sit and get to know us. We'll buy you a drink."

A Fragile Wife

Caden went with her to the couch she and Ken shared. Within moments they bought him another beer, and within minutes they were talking about the club, what they did, and sharing enough information to make things pleasant but without going into strange lands. Lana was familiar with this pattern. She and Ken had picked up enough subs over the years to make this a seamless transition from conversation to bedroom, assuming their intended didn't bail on them. *That sometimes happens.* Came with the territory of being a swinging couple who wanted to do nothing but party and have a lot of sex with as many people as possible.

"What do you think, Bunny?" Ken asked fifteen minutes in, when Caden got up to briefly excuse himself to the restroom. That was either code for "See you!" or "I need to get ready for this bullshit." They would find out soon enough. "The man is your type of sub."

"If you mean hairless, muscular, and obedient, then you may be right, Husband."

"I am usually right about these things, Wife."

"Hmm."

"Love," Ken growled, wrapping his arm tightly around her, his words diving right into her ear and plummeting to her loins. "I want to see that man's cock in every hole you'll let him."

"You have *such* a way with words, Kenny." Yet Lana smiled, titillated. Caden was certainly handsome. Easily controlled. He would do about anything they said, and Lana already knew what she would tell him to do. *Fuck me wide open for my husband.* Her thighs tightened, but it wasn't in fear. If she got aroused enough, she would be more than ready to take on that anaconda. They didn't bite, after all.

No, they just choked and strangled. *Fantastic mental image.* And any hole she would allow would basically mean her pussy and mouth. *I might choke on it after all.*

"I like him," she said, projecting an aura of confidence. That was easy. Following through sometimes, on the other hand, could present a problem to a woman like Lana. "I would fuck him."

"Would? Or will?"

"Whatever you want, Kenny."

"What I *want* Bunny…" He bit her ear, sending so many shudders through her body that she thought she would come right there. "Is to watch that man take on that little pussy of yours. Or would it be the other way around?"

"If he's good, then it would be a very mutual endeavor. As you know, dear husband who has fucked me a thousand times, it takes two to make a good, clean entrance in there."

"I'll do my best to make sure you are properly ready."

"If you touch me, it would be as my sub. Otherwise that guy won't stay hard."

"I have a *hard* time believing that. One look at you makes me hard."

"That's *you,* though. You're not some run of the mill sub running around here looking for pussy to put him in his place."

"Thank God. I think that would get tiring after a while at my age. I'm not twenty-two like our young friend… who is coming back now."

They finished their drinks. Ken got up to find an assistant to help them get a room, and Lana went into Domme overdrive.

"Caden, sweetheart," she said, joining him on his loveseat and putting her hand on his bare shoulder. "Tell me you want what I'm offering you."

"I do, Mistress."

"Good. As soon as my husband gets back, we'll take this show on the road." She tipped Caden's chin toward her and kissed him.

It wasn't a gentle peck. It wasn't even flirting. Lana was going to eat this brute alive, so help her God. Not just up top... nope. She was going to inhale him through every orifice that could stand it. She would do it for herself... and she would do it for her kinky husband, wherever he was.

Caden was the type of kisser who deferred to her strength. And Lana had a lot of strength, especially when it came to turning her husband on. Like now, when he reappeared behind her, rubbing her shoulder and whispering that he had a key with their names on it.

Lana took the lead. After all, she was the one in charge of this situation. *Why am I so into this?* Usually she would be nervous. She knew how much it could potentially hurt – but also feel good. *It's because I really do want to cuckold my husband.* She was into the idea of forcing him to watch her take on another man. A man she picked up and decided to fuck, with or without him. This husband of hers – the one who was possibly cheating on her – wouldn't know what to do with himself with the tables turned. How would Ken *really* react to Caden doing his wife? That would tell her a lot more than an unreliable witness like Roberta the chef.

"Look at you," Ken said, taking his wife into his arms the moment they entered the private room. Caden lingered in the hallway, nodding to other couples and singles passing by, some of them lethargic from lovemaking and others giddy with anticipation. It was that kind of energy that made Lana so bubbly in places like The Dark Hour. "You're the hottest woman in this club. And I'm going to watch you own that."

Lana pushed him toward a chair on the side of the room. "Sit down," she commanded. Ken landed with a huff, his eyes fixated on her figure. "Now be a good boy and watch your wife work." *And be worked.* She didn't remind her husband of that.

Caden entered, shutting the door behind him.

"You," Lana said, snapping her fingers and pointing to the plain bed in the middle of the dimly lit room. "There."

This should've been one of the hottest nights of the year. And it would've been, if Lana's worries weren't hanging over her. She looked at her husband, as she sat on the edge of the bed with Caden, wondering what he was *really* thinking. Did he mean what he said about her being the hottest woman in the club? Probably. That didn't mean he thought she was the hottest woman in the world. Or maybe he did. That still didn't mean he wasn't going elsewhere for other hot women.

Well, now it was Lana's turn to change those tides. She knew how to work her husband. She knew what he liked to see...

A Fragile Wife

She went into this situation determined to have sex despite her husband. Or maybe in spite of him! Yet as she pulled Caden to her, she caught a glimpse of Ken in his chair, smoking his electronic cigarette and giving her a look that said, *"You're hot, honey. Glad I married you."*

All the ice around her heart melted. Lana saw the man she loved. The man she wanted to keep pleasing. The man she was afraid of losing, whether through design or through her own machinations.

"Keep your hands off me." Before, Lana was ready to rub herself all over this man, to give her husband a taste of his own supposed medicine. But when she felt that tug at her heart, she no longer wanted Caden as a person. She wanted him as a *body*. Lana was telling the truth when she said she wanted a man with one function only. Well, she would damn well treat him that way. And knowing most male subs around that club, he would love it as long as he got what he ultimately wanted.

Her.

A few curt words.

Everything in between.

Sex.

Lana didn't offer any paddles, crops, whips, or cock rings. She did, however, offer a scenario that made most men she encountered too excited to bear. Hence the hard cock she encountered when she opened those tight jeans and unleashed the very thing that made her legs push together.

"Well, look at this." Lana had no shame grabbing Caden's shaft and showing off his ridiculous erection. The man wasn't

Cynthia Dane

just well endowed. He was a behemoth. Even the most hardened Domme would raise her eyebrows and get out extra lube from looking at that thing.

And Caden knew he had something *unusual.* He grinned at the way Lana looked at him. He even spared Ken a glance, the man with a perfect poker face. What he thought of Caden and what he was going to do to the woman of the room? Not even Lana was 100% sure anymore.

"You're a big boy, aren't you?" While Lana cooed in her new man's ear, she sent the old one a signal they had used a hundred times over the years: she held up her left hand, wrapping her other hand around it and gesturing until Ken reached into the condom bowl and tossed his wife one. "You wanna fuck me with that cock, Big Boy?"

Whether sub or Dom, men couldn't keep themselves from smirking like they owned the universe when women asked them that question. "If it pleases you, Mistress."

"Not just me. You need to please my husband too. He wants to see me fuck huge cock. You'll see why soon enough. First…" She unbuttoned the front of her blouse, letting her breasts fall free from their casements so the warm, inviting air perked her nipples and let her feel a new wave of arousal through her body. She would need all the inspiration she could get. "You need to please me and get me wet. Can you do that, Big Boy?'

She spent this whole time stroking his length, in awe over how big he grew in those few moments. *This man could be a porn star.* Shave him all clean and pretty, fluff him off set, and then

- 150 -

sick him on a little hot young thing who had a pre-stretched pussy. *That's not me.* The idea made the whole situation hotter. Caden could have any woman he wanted with this monster. Yet he decided to go with Lana... *and* her husband. Even if the men never touched, there was no denying that they were both a part of this experience.

"You got it all under control, hon?" Ken asked from his chair. He continued to smoke, his eyes never leaving his wife's form. *I can feel his adoration from here.* The feeling she felt for over ten years now. Maybe he really did still love her that much...

"Control? I always have everything under control." Lana ran her hands across her nipples and then Caden's hard, strong chest. *Ah, youth.* "I'm not opposed to you egging me on, though, dearest husband."

"I always knew you loved the sound of my voice."

Lana leaned down, licking her fingers and wetting the head of Caden's cock. *Whelp, time to break my jaw.* "Don't be a stranger over there."

What Caden thought of this... who cared? The man was about to get a blowjob from an aggressive woman. He had nothing to complain about.

"Look at you go," Ken said in a soft drawl. "Nobody sucks cock like my beautiful wife."

Spurred on by her husband's comment, Lana sucked on the tip of Caden's cock. "And look at my husband," she murmured on another man's dick. "Watching his wife play the whore."

"Honey, when my cock is a rod in my pants, you can be as loose as you damn well please."

Cynthia Dane

She dared him. "And when your cock *isn't* a rod?" Caden's scent was starting to get overwhelming, which was distracting, since Lana wanted to concentrate on her husband's presence.

"Even when it's not a rod, baby."

Sure.

"Fuck," Caden groaned, his hips thrusting slightly upward as Lana attempted to take more of his thick girth into her mouth. "I mean... forgive me, Mistress."

"She's busy," Ken barked. "Be quiet."

Be still, my loins. Even when she was also in charge, she could never get enough of Ken's Dom voice. It made her bolder, opening her mouth to take in as much as she could.

It hurt. It was uncomfortable. But it was so hot that she knew she didn't want to do anything else right now.

"That's right, baby. Take that man's cock."

Oh, she would. She could only go down halfway, but by then Caden had filled her mouth and half her throat. *This is so ridiculous.* Her hand wrapped around the base of the man's shaft, squeezing, stroking, trying to get him to the point of coming but not quite. *He better not blow his load before I fuck him...*

Before she could do that, she had to make sure she was wet enough. As she sucked, stroked, and pushed her body to strange limits, Lana reached between her legs and tested her current state of arousal. It had begun, but was nowhere near where it needed to be.

Ken must have noticed this as well, for he said, "You are so hot, Lana. When they say the word maneater, they are talking about you, in every sense of it."

A Fragile Wife

His deep voice sent liquid down her fingers. Lana pressed one into her slit, touching her clit and feeling shivers take her over. She sent her husband, still sitting as if he were the most disinterested man in the world, a glare that would hopefully encourage him to continue.

"How did I get so lucky having a woman like you for my wife? It's ridiculous how perfect you are for me. Not only are you absolutely stunning, but you share all of my appetites. You're strong, you're resilient, you don't take any shit when it's flung at you. Watching you scare men into submission, literally and figuratively, is the hottest thing alive. Whether I'm letting you on top of me or slamming my cock into you from behind, all I can think about is how much I love you and want to do this forever."

She believed him. That belief not only made her quiver from head to toe, but it made her lift her lips from Caden and say, "Do you wanna take me right now, Kenneth? While I devour this huge cock?"

"Do I? Fuck, yes. I want to pull you onto my cock while you suck that guy's. I want to see that pretty outfit and hair in the most exquisite spit roast in the world. We'd live like kings."

Lana laughed. Caden wasn't laughing. He was leaning back, dying from the oral stimulation his Mistress provided.

"Except I won't right now. Because I want you a very specific way before I take you. I want to see that stranger you barely know fuck you wide open. I want to see the sweet agony on your face as you struggle to take that ridiculous thing."

Cynthia Dane

Why am I so wet? Normally this kind of banter didn't get her *this* wet. Not as much as performing for her husband did. Yet there was something in Ken's voice, in his words and mannerisms – or lack thereof – that made her so damn hot that she could barely control herself. She wanted to slip one, two fingers into her body, fucking herself until she came, moaning uncontrollably on this man. Not very practical, however. Especially when she had other things to accomplish that night.

That still didn't explain why she felt the way she did.

Because he's dominating me. That realization settled in like a plague in her mind. She may be controlling Caden, but Ken was controlling *her*. This was his scenario. His fantasy.

This all played into the mind games he orchestrated.

He wanted to see his wife, Lana, be debased and God knew what else with this total stranger with a huge dick she couldn't take on most nights, let alone tonight.

He wanted to hear her cry out in pleasure, in pain. He wanted to watch her go to another plane of existence, with or without him. For the love of all that was good and pure, Ken Andrews wanted to watch his wife *get* fucked, not fuck!

There was a difference. A difference Lana was apparently more than ready to play into as she felt arousal drip down her fingers. She was as ready as she was going to get.

"All right, Big Boy," she said, sitting up and slapping the inside of Caden's thigh. "You've been so good and such a perfect sport. It's time for you to claim your prize."

A Fragile Wife

Before she could draw her knees onto the bed and get into position, however, her husband ripped off his tie and tossed it to her. "He doesn't get to look at you," he said. "Only I do."

Quivers. *Quivers.*

"Yes, sir," she whispered.

"That's my girl."

His girl. Even now, so many years later, it sometimes felt too good to be true. How could this man be so in love with her? Was it real? Lana didn't often believe in fate, but if such a thing brought her together with her husband, than she was willing to trust it for at least one more night.

Tonight, she belonged to him. She didn't need a collar or wedding vows to prove that to herself and the world.

I want to please him. I want acceptance. Lana looped her husband's tie around Caden's face, blindfolding him. At this point, Caden would agree to about anything, let alone a little sensory deprecation. The moment the man could no longer see her, Lana ripped open the condom package… and laughed.

"Excuse me, *sir*," she said, tossing the unused condom into the trash across the room. *I should've been a basketball player.* "You are seriously underestimating this man."

Ken reached into the condom bowl again, this time pulling out a bigger size. "I was hoping you would say that."

How many women could say they had a husband who found this hot? How many husbands wouldn't get jealous? Whether of their wife being with another man… or how big that man was? Ken had never worn an XL condom before,

Cynthia Dane

Lana was pretty sure. Didn't stop him from lusting after the image of his wife taking an XL dick.

"I knew you would like this," Lana muttered, rolling the latex down Caden's long cock. "All right, Big Boy," she said, louder. "You've got one job. Fuck me."

"Yes, Mistress."

"I said *be quiet.*"

The fact both Ken and Lana said it at the same time surprised no one.

Caden wasn't here as a third wheel. He wasn't even a person in this moment. He was a tool, full stop. A tool that lived to serve and be used.

Which was good. Because there was only one man Lana answered to at all, in any situation... and he was sitting a meager few feet away, vapor curling around his head as he watched his wife get on her hands and knees, facing him.

She could have given him a side view. She could have given him the porn treatment and let him see as much penetration as possible. *I want to look into his eyes.* Lana's fingers curled around the edge of the bed as she opened her legs and felt Caden situate himself behind her. *Because he's looking right into mine.* This was their moment, as husband and wife.

Poor Caden. He had no idea what he was dealing with, emotionally... or physically.

"Ah!" Lana had half a mind to turn around and swat the man trying to push his thick dick into her. "Watch it!"

Funny thing, being a woman of her standing in this situation. At some point she had to transform from Caden's

Domme to her husband's sub. And that moment came when Caden pushed one inch in, Lana's body stretching its damndest in order to accommodate something it was *not* used to.

Her body had to relax. She had to mind over matter the situation. She was Lana Andrews. People knew she could handle anything that came her way. What was one measly cock?

"That's it, baby." Ken's voice kept her grounded through this tiresome scene. *Good, because this hurts.* Lana sucked in her breath and willed herself wider, feeling this other man's heavy cock slowly slide into her. "Relax and take it. You're so beautiful."

He said that, but Lana didn't feel very beautiful. She felt ridiculous, her knees sinking deep into the bed as her knuckles turned white enough to scare a doctor. The only way she was getting through the initial burst of discomfort was by regulating her breathing and focusing on her husband not so far away.

He was her rock. And now? He was the man getting off on watching his wife turn into the type of woman she begged him to call her during sex.

"Does it feel good?" Ken asked, putting his electronic cigarette away. "Does your pussy like being packed, Wife?"

She tried to speak, but the words wouldn't come out as anything more than a whimper. Caden was squeezing her ass, pulling his cock out and feeling how stretched she was with his fingers. Lana bent down, head scraping the bed. Feeling a strange man's fingers inside her, forcing her open so she could take his cock, was almost too much to bear.

Cynthia Dane

When Caden tried again, the tip of his cock burrowing farther this time, Lana let out an unfamiliar cry. *Oh my God. Oh my God.* The smirk on Ken's face humbled her.

This was for him. This wasn't necessarily about her pleasure, but his. And Lana thrived with that knowledge.

"Yes!" she shouted, fingers grabbing sheets as she forced her hips back, attempting to take more of Caden's cock. She was opening. Not a lot, but enough to take a little more of him as the seconds passed. He would pull out, let her get wet again, and then slide in again. It got easier each time, but no less intrusive, no less intense. Lana did not have a body meant for taking men of this size, but she would do her damndest to do it – and enjoy it.

"Good girl," Ken said softly. "Take that man's cock. All the way, honey."

He didn't have to tell her that. From the moment Caden started sliding into her, easier than ever, Lana became determined to feel his damned balls slap against her ass.

She didn't expect it to be *easy* because she was.

"Fuck my wife, sub," Ken said. "She's been a naughty girl and deserves to have her pussy torn in two. You're the lucky man to do it."

Lana would have told him to piss off, but now was not the time.

Instead, she said, "Do you like this, Ken? You like watching me take on some stranger's big dick?"

"Always, love."

He said it too easily. As if that disinterested façade wasn't a façade at all, but how he really felt right now. *Fuck that.* "It feels good," she whimpered, and she did not lie. Even through the discomfort, she felt that relieving pleasure of a woman accepting a man into her body. It was sexual, yes, but also so liberating. She was high on the life this man passed on to her. High on the need to have him fuck her brains out, to give her an experience she had never felt before.

Namely, turning her into a vessel of her husband's pleasure – and he wasn't even touching her.

When Caden "broke" through, groaning in relief as he pushed himself in as deep as physically allowed, Lana gave herself over to nothing but sex. She retreated into herself, knees buckling against the bed, breath heavy, heavier, heaviest when Caden pulled out, thrust back in, and made her scream into the sheets.

The man's strong hands held her hips to his, thrusting into her, long, cruel strokes of his cock that opened her beyond her limits. *I'm going to be so loose after this.* That's what Ken wanted. He *wanted* to see his wife's gaping pussy after another man had been inside her. It got him off to think of Lana as a commodity to be passed around, to relive a part of that gangbang she always told him about. *This doesn't even compare. This is one man and his huge erection.* None of the men in that frat came close to this. She would have died.

"Oh, *God,*" she moaned, hands splayed against the sheets as Caden began to go at her earnestly. Steady rhythms filled her body, Caden grunting like a beast as he rammed himself into

Cynthia Dane

her, over and over, making her feel more and more like her husband's disposable whore.

She went into this situation feeling confident and sensual. Now she had a brief moment of panic, wondering what her husband *really* thought.

"Ken!" she cried, not struggling against Caden for all her worry. She sat up, letting the man fuck her, his cock swelling in preparation of orgasm. *Oh God no, I can't handle that...* "Kenny..."

"What is it, baby? You're so hot right now."

"Really?" Her lip trembled. Nipples brushed against the sheets in this position, and before Lana knew it, pleasure began to spread. Euphoria took root in her brain, making it more pleasing than ever to look into her husband's stoic visage as his fingers clenched against his thighs. "You like this?"

"I do, Bunny." He rarely said that name in front of other people. For him to say it now meant he really didn't consider Caden as a human entity. He was a tool, indeed. A tool drilling his wife. "I love watching you with other men, especially if they make you look like this."

"Like what?"

He bared his teeth in a wide, menacing smile. "Like a sex drunk harlot who can't say no to any cock who comes her way. You're mine, Bunny, but that doesn't mean I want to be your only one. Know what I mean?"

She did, and she didn't. But she couldn't think too hard about it. Caden fucked her, nearly raw, pulling out long enough to let her get all wet again before slamming back into her. She screamed to feel him leave her and then fill her again.

All Lana cared about now was pleasing her husband. Visually pleasing. Emotionally pleasing. She existed to be his one and only, even if he wanted nothing to do with her right now. *Come back to me, baby.* Her words evaporated from her throat as she braced herself against Caden's fucking,

"Ken," she whined, forcing her head up so she could see her husband's face. "Am I pleasing you?"

"Yes, Bunny. You're pleasing me very much."

Relief flooded her as orgasm began to claim her. The man hadn't even touched her clit, and the size of him alone was enough to make her come already.

"Do you think I'm pretty?"

The only sounds in the room were the squeak of the bed, the grunts in Caden's throat, and his cock taking Lana. Skin on skin had never sounded so intoxicating.

"You're gorgeous, Lana."

She almost sobbed into the bed.

"Come for me, baby. Come on that man's cock."

He didn't have to ask twice. Before Lana could process *he thinks I'm beautiful and he loves me* climax was overtaking her, expanding in her veins, heating her skin, and turning her into a crazed woman who only cared about one thing.

Her cries of pleasure echoed in the room. Her inner walls refused to let Caden leave her, holding him within her as she began to milk the seed from his body.

"Holy shit," he muttered. "You're so tight, Mistress."

He had no idea yet.

Caden's orgasm took Lana to a new height of desire. *I'm going to…* She didn't know what. Die? Maybe. Come again? Definitely. Just as her first orgasm abated, a new one began, ripping through her body, making her writhe, and nearly sending her over the edge of the bed.

"Fuck me!" Lana cried. "*Fuck me and come!*"

She felt the heat, but she didn't feel the seed. Ripples of Caden's orgasm passed to her, the man containing his groans to mere whispers. He pushed her into the bed, holding up her skirt, pushing his hand against her ass, and stilling his cock deep within her as he emptied himself in front of Lana's voyeuristic husband.

"Good,' Ken said. "That's exactly what I wanted to see."

Lana crashed from her high as quickly as she ascended it. Worn out and used up, she collapsed onto the bed, her aching legs pulling to the side as she gingerly closed her thighs. A certain soreness took her over… but she was so relieved to hear her husband's words that she didn't even pay it any mind.

As she stayed in her fuzzy, post-coital reverie, she heard Ken's voice say something curt to Caden. The man got off the bed. By the time Lana returned to her senses, she and Ken were alone in their borrowed room.

Her husband sat on the edge of the bed, stroking the errant hairs falling out of Lana's tight bun. She gravitated to his after care, putting all her love, trust, and need into him as she crawled into his lap and moaned in relief.

"You were terrific, Bunny," he said gently, massaging the back of her neck and stroking the length of her spine. "I hope you're not in too much pain. Need me to do anything?"

She wrapped her arms beneath her head, content to live in his lap. "Just be right here."

Ken sat, rubbing her back, her shoulders, and cupping the back of her head with his hand. For a while, neither of them said anything. Why would they have to when they were perfectly capable of saying everything that needed to be said with their body language and heavy breaths?

"I love you," Ken finally said, his hands holding her shoulders. "I rarely see this side of you. I must be the only man to ever see it."

She lifted her head. "I love you too."

Lana nearly cried, for no other reason than she was afraid. Afraid of losing him. Afraid of not being good enough. Afraid that she could not keep her husband's interests beyond this private room.

Was it too much to ask for those reassurances?

"What do you want?" she asked softly, fingers clinging to his shirt. "I'll give you anything."

"Anything?"

"Yes, I'll…" Her throat went dry, her eyes darting around the room in search of something else to focus on. "I'll give you my heart, Kenny. I love you so much, it doesn't seem fair that I ask so much of you."

"You don't, really."

"Do you want my soul? I'll give it to you, baby. It isn't worth all that much."

"Don't say that."

"Do you want my body?"

Ken bit his lip. "I do."

Lana placed her hand in his lap, feeling the erection he maintained from watching his wife with another man. "I'll do whatever you want." She started to unzip him, but Ken stopped her.

"No, my love. You know what I really want."

Of course. It was what he mentioned out in the maw of the club. What he *really* wanted was to see what was done by another man.

Before, Lana would have said she didn't really understand what turned her husband on in this situation. So what if she rolled onto her back, opened her legs, and watched as Ken pulled aside her folds? By now, she was returning to normal, although enough wetness remained behind for another man to have his way with her. It wouldn't be the first time she took her husband after hosting another man inside her body.

And yet this felt very, *very* different.

She wanted so badly to be exactly what he wanted. *Before,* she wouldn't have given a shit if Ken was less than impressed. Now? The only thing that mattered was being good enough for her husband to drop his zipper, loom between her legs, and take her for himself.

A Fragile Wife

"Ow," Lana muttered, although she wanted this. She wanted to feel her body taken over again, this time by the man she loved almost unconditionally. "Be gentle?"

He was, in his own way.

Oh, he was gentle in how he treated her between the legs, knowing that she was still sore and needed tenderness above all else. Yet his intensity as he made love to her, his eyes boring into hers as he made her his over and over again, was something beyond a man like Caden could have ever hoped to give her. *Because this is my husband.* Her partner. Her Master. Her good boy when the time was right. Tonight, he was a little bit of everything, and most definitely the man who loved her more than anyone else could have.

"That's right, Lana," he growled, as his wife relaxed around him. "You're all mine."

Ken took her hands and lifted them above her head, thrusting into her gently, but with renewed purpose. He would continuously remind her that no other man made love to her like he did. And if he couldn't do that? Then he wasn't a man worthy of having her affection.

Although she did not come again, he did, quickly, spending himself with a few bursts of controlling pleasure. Not once did his eyes waver from hers.

Lana felt small, but loved.

"My God," Ken muttered, lying next to her when he was finished. He watched as his seed spilled from his wife and onto the otherwise clean sheets. "As the universe intended."

Yes, baby, I'm all yours. There was no doubt about it. All Lana continued to worry about was that Ken was all hers. If a wife didn't have that, then what *did* she have?

Soon, she thought. Soon everything would sort itself out. It had to.

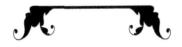

Chapter 11

"Do You Believe Me?"

There was nothing like coming home on a rainy evening after a long day hassling investors and threatening to cut off a few balls if Lana didn't get her way. Ken had to remain in town to finish up some paperwork, so Lana summoned her driver and went home, far away from the ruckus. She looked forward to a quiet dinner and lounging in her room, playing music, enjoying the fire, and organizing her makeup case.

If her husband managed to get his ass home at a reasonable time, even better. Maybe they could soak in the bath together.

Of course, Lana was not so lucky. The first person she encountered upon entering her spacious home was none other than Chloe, who appeared to take Lana's coat and umbrella.

"Did you have a good day, ma'am?" she asked, her cute little face almost enough to make Lana throw up. "Roberta says your dinner is waiting for you."

Lana eyed her suspiciously. "Bring it up to my room." She shook off her sweater and piled it on top of her coat in Chloe's arms. "If my husband comes home, tell him I want to see him." They had a cuddle appointment.

"Yes, ma'am."

Lana hoped that was the last of seeing any help that night. As soon as she had her dinner waiting for her on a small table in the master suite, she switched on one of her favorite TV shows and enjoyed it until she was full and happy enough to go about her business.

She slipped into something more comfortable, which amounted to a thin white T-shirt and cotton shorts, topped with a red silk robe that was more style than function. It mattered little to her. Her body ached from the trials of the day, and if her damned husband would respond to her texts, she could find out if she should take a bath without him or wait for his arrival.

Damnit, forgot my seal. She was in the midst of gluing invitations together for a soiree she was throwing at the beginning of February, shortly after returning from her second honeymoon. She paused the DVR on the flat screen and shuffled into the hallway. Her office was a few doors down, and she was absolutely sure that's where she last left her seal.

A Fragile Wife

Unfortunately, Ken's office was another stone's throw away from *her* office. This meant she had a fantastic view of his open door and the light spilling out.

He's home? That was annoying, if only because he never texted her, and nobody came up to inform her after she explicitly asked for them to do so. *I need to hire new help. And a new husband.* Huffing, Lana marched down the hall, bypassing her office to head straight to Ken's.

She caught Chloe going through her husband's locked drawer. A key dangled from her fingers.

"What the!" Lana suddenly became three times as large, overtaking the doorway the moment Chloe freaked the hell out. She slammed the desk drawer shut, locking it with no more finality than Ken ever did. "What the hell is going on here?"

They came to an instant impasse. Lana, finding the help going through her husband's belongings; Chloe, caught with a key hanging from her hand. Her face was so pale that she looked almost spectral.

"Mrs. Andrews…"

"That's *right*." Lana found her bearings and approached, not giving a shit if her robe slipped open and Chloe saw the boss's bouncing tits beneath a T-shirt. "Mrs. Fucking Andrews. Care to tell me what the *fuck* you are doing here, little girl?"

Chloe really did look little and girlish. She looked like a teenager caught sneaking out, or a small child caught peeking a look at the gifts beneath the Christmas Tree. But she *wasn't* a child. She was a grown-ass woman. A grown, sexualized woman caught going through the master's belongings.

Or had that key been *given* to her? Not even Lana had a key to her husband's desk. She knew where to find it, but had never been *given* one…

"I'm so sorry… Mr. Andrews told me to…"

"Told you to what? Oh, I bet this is rich." Here it was. Here came the confession. Chloe couldn't deny it any longer. Either she was up to something too nefarious for words, or she was cheating with Lana's bastard of a husband.

"He told me to pick up and drop things off here. I've been helping him with a project, ma'am."

"What project?"

"I'm so sorry!"

Lana was no match for how tiny this girl was. Chloe was able to slip easily past her, bolting into the hallway with the key still clasped in her hand. No matter how loudly Lana called after her, she could not convince the girl to stop, confess her sins, and meet her fate.

You're kidding me!

Lana went into her husband's office, slamming the door behind her. *I will expose this asshole.* She went to the coat closet full of tax files and receipts. There, on the top shelf, was an inconspicuous box that Ken kept some valuables in. Sure enough, she quickly found a tiny ring of keys, one of which was sure to go to his desk.

I may regret this, but I don't care. Lana tried one key after the other, crouched low between desk and office chair. No matter which key she tried, however, nothing was making the lock budge.

A Fragile Wife

Not until she reached the second to last key, which snapped everything open.

Lana gasped, mentally preparing herself for whatever she might find. Love letters? Dirty books? Presents exchanged between master and mistress? Whatever was in here, it was not meant for Lana's eyes... but for some reason Chloe was more than invited to partake.

That was enough to give Lana the strength to pry it open.

She looked upon a mess of books and papers. Neatly organized, yes, but a mess nonetheless. Piles of Ken's stationery, neatly covered in his handwriting, stared back at her. Spiral bound books and what looked like a manuscript proof were crammed into the corner. Everything was covered in colorful sticky notes, some of them with Ken's handwriting, and others with what looked like... Chloe's.

What the fuck? Lana pulled out the top stack of papers. They were neatly creased in the middle, the perfect size of Chloe's bag that she packed around the house when she went about her job. They even smelled like her, if that was possible. Sure enough, Lana found a pink sticky note on top written in girly handwriting. *"This is really beautiful!!!"*

"I'll show her a beautiful bruise..." Lana ripped off the note, crumpled it in her hand, and began reading the sordid love letter her husband wrote the maid.

"The first time I met my wife, I thought I was crushed by the weight of the universe and sent to the afterlife. That's because she looked like a glamorous angel come to deliver either good or bad news about my soul's fate. Instead, she came up to me and asked if I knew where the women's

restroom was. She was one of the only women there, which should have tipped me off regarding how deliriously intelligent and bullheaded she is."

What the hell?

"Lana Losers was definitely not a loser, no matter how much people made fun of her for her name or for being a woman, let alone a conventionally beautiful one. She was a winner through and through. In that first hour meeting her, I learned that she had dominated her internship at one of the biggest real estate agencies in the city. There were vicious rumors that she slept her way to the position. These are lies, meant to slander my wife. But, even if she had, it didn't demean her in any way to me. She proved her merit when she showed me her portfolio of one-hundred high class sales... all within the past year!"

Lana flipped through the first half of the papers. Her name showed up at least once on every single one of them.

"What. The. *Fuck.*"

She reached back in and pulled out more papers. *"For our wedding, Lana wanted to have only three bridesmaids, which pleased my mother greatly, since I have exactly three brothers. However, the drama that erupted because I chose two friends over two of my brothers almost caused us to elope in Vegas. I brought it up more than once. It would have been easy enough to do... hop a plane and get married at the nearest Elvis Station. Yet I knew how much a family affair meant to my wife, and convinced her to take on two more bridesmaids. She ended up picking a pair of cousins she hadn't talked to since she was nineteen. I think they thought they had stepped into Cinderella's castle on our wedding day. I couldn't blame them. I thought she looked like a princess as well."*

Lana fell to her knees in front of the open drawer. There were more pages – pages upon pages – with Ken's meticulous handwriting scribbling his thoughts on his wife, marriage, and even bits and pieces about his career and home life. *"The first thing she told me when I asked her to be my girlfriend was that she didn't want to have children. Was I okay with that? Would I pressure her in ten years to give me an heir? You have to understand, if you're not in our society, it can be confusing… but women don't have a lot of freedom regarding children. It's mandatory in many of the more conservative families to have an heir, preferably a boy or two. You know the saying – an heir and a spare. Lana was upfront saying she was going to get her tubes tied or ablated, or whatever, and never consider motherhood again. It wasn't for her. Until then, I had been on the fence about children, assuming that my wife would make the final decision. Well, she did, didn't she? I wouldn't take a gaggle of perfect children in exchange for my wife."*

More words. More praise. Tiny criticisms, like how she often spat her toothpaste into the sink and didn't wash it down all the way. Or how she mumbled in her sleep, usually about the most nonsensical things. *"She can be harsh to our staff sometimes, but she's also very generous come Christmas and birthdays, or because something made her think of someone working in our house or office. Lana simply expects excellence from everyone around her. If any of our staff thinks she's tough on them, imagine how she is on me! If I screw something up, I hear about it for months, sometimes years. She wants me to improve myself. In turn, I challenge her as well."*

Sometimes things were crossed out. Other times there were tiny notes in the margins, usually in Chloe's curly handwriting. *"You're so sweet, Mr. Andrews." "I'm not sure Mrs. Andrews would like the word 'beastly' in reference to her flirting…" "Do you have a*

Cynthia Dane

picture to go with this passage? I think the audience would like a visual reference. I know I do!"

"Lana!"

Papers crumpled in her hands as Lana turned, heart thumping wildly in her chest. "Ken!"

There he stood, in his office doorway, suit jacket tossed over his arm and tie loose around his neck. The look he gave his wife was both one of shock and horror. "What are you doing in my private drawer?"

Lana dropped what she held, but the damage was already done. She and her husband kept few secrets between them, but one thing they acknowledged was private correspondence and spaces. They didn't go through each other's mail, electronic or physical. They didn't intrude on meetings unless previously given permission. And they sure as hell stayed out of each other's locked drawers. Lana had violated more than her husband's trust by rooting through his locked desk drawer.

"I had to know what was going on!" Already she was on the defensive, determined to clear her besmirched name before her husband even *had* the chance to besmirch it. "Things had been so shady around here... you and Chloe..."

"What about me and Chloe?"

She saw the look on her husband's face. He knew instantly what she had suspected, and it was more than betrayal coloring his cheekbones. Lana bent over the yellow stationery scattered on the floor... and cried.

They were tears of relief and fear. Relief that her paranoia was just that, and her husband was not cheating on her. But the

- 174 -

fear. The fear! *I fucked up badly!* Now Ken knew how crazy she was. Not only had she suspected something as heinous as infidelity, but she had rooted through his private stashes in search of something against him. Had the tables been turned? Lana would have never forgiven him.

Ken stayed far away from her for a minute. Lana could not see his face through her shameful tears, but she could feel his aura from so far away. *"How could you, Lana?"* He wasn't angry. He was sad. The woman he had written so highly of in these papers was sobbing on his office floor after being caught like Chloe was.

"Lana." That stern voice was not sexual. *Rarely* did Lana hear this side of him and not be the submissive end to his domination. No, this was matrimonial, sure, but for all the wrong reasons. "I am not sleeping with our maid."

"I know!" she cried through her sobs, each one more heinous than the last. They wracked her body… a body purging itself of the negativity, the paranoia, and her will to destroy a marriage that seemed too good to be true for so long. And yet here she was, destroying the best thing that had ever happened to her. "I'm sorry."

Sorry would never be enough for her unwarranted suspicions. Of course Ken had not cheated on her. *Why* would he? Was she really so dumb, so foolhardy as to believe this man who let her get away with murder would be any less than faithful to a fault? For fuck's sake, they were *swingers!* If he was happy, why would he cheat? Because he was a man? Because men always cheated? What sort of disgusting half-truths had

Lana swallowed over the years? Did she really have so little faith in her marriage?

I didn't confront him about the maid because deep down I knew it was baseless. Like her therapist told her, she had only been concerned with dismantling her own marriage, finding every little fault as an excuse to get a divorce. Except to what end? Did she really need Ken to prove his love to her every ten years? Would she still be playing this game with herself at *eighty?*

"I can't believe you went through my things." Now he came to her, swiftly, his polished leather shoes appearing beside her huddling, shaking body.

"I had to know…" It was all she could say. "I had to know what you were up to. Everyone was being so secretive, I couldn't take it anymore!"

"You didn't even ask me?"

"How could I have…" What? Trusted him? Lana cut off that thought before she completely embarrassed herself even further. "I wanted to see it for myself. Kenneth…" She held up the tattered papers. "What *is* this?"

He bent down, hands snatching the papers away and putting them back in neat order. "A manuscript." The papers slid back into his desk drawer, where he plucked out one of the bound proofs and held it above his wife's head. "I wrote a book. A memoir."

"What?"

Her tears had abated. Now she saw her husband through puffy eyes. She saw a man disappointed with himself, his wife, and whatever this project was that he held in his hands. "It was going to be a surprise, Bunny." It surprised Lana to hear her nickname. "I was going to show you this proof while we were on our honeymoon. It's being published in a couple of months."

Lana couldn't believe her ears. "A *memoir?*" She didn't even know Kenneth wrote outside of legal documents and the occasional note to somebody. The man had their personal assistant at work transcribe most of his letters. "Since when have you been writing a memoir?"

"Since a year ago. One of my old college buddies is a publisher in New York. He approached me saying he wanted to do a line of memoirs from successful businessmen and women. He was interested in you writing one too, or us writing one together, but I suggested I write one *about* you, in a way. He agreed. Now here I am, the biggest fool in the universe."

"You're not…"

"I must be, for not foreseeing this. If I hadn't been wearing my blinders that said this should be a surprise… I should have told you about it the moment I finished the first draft."

"And Chloe?"

"Chloe?" Ken laughed. "She was one of my first readers. All the others, including the editor, were men. I wanted a woman's view. Who else would I have asked if not you? Roberta?"

"The package…"

"…That I got by the pool that day? Forget it all, Lana, that was the proof! I didn't want you to see it yet."

"And those letters from you were really your handwritten drafts…" Holy shit. She was terrible. "And you gave her a key to your desk so she could…"

"…Put back what she finished commenting on and take out the next parts. Yes. I wanted to change the lock anyway, and was going to after this project was finished. It won't matter if she makes a copy of the key, because it won't work in a few months anyway." Ken snorted. "Apparently I need to find a new hiding spot for my keys."

"I'm so sorry!" Lana was on the verge of tears again. "I don't know what's wrong with me."

She couldn't hold back the drops falling from her eyes. She tasted salt. Bitter. Sour. Everything was sent up from her heart for the sole purpose of making her throw up.

"Ken…"

He put a hand on her shoulder. Tender. *Firm.* "I don't know what to say, Lana. I never in a million years expected this from you."

And never in a million years did Lana expect to snort at a statement like that. "Are you kidding? You know better than anyone what a vindictive bitch I am. I was ready to rip out that girl's entrails and parade them in front of you!"

"You should probably go apologize to her. At least now I know why she's being so skittish around us. Besides…" He nicked his finger against her chin. "I do know how vindictive you can be. Don't think of it as being vindictive, though. It's kind of hot that you're possessive…"

"No it's not. It's messed up. I…" Finally, she forced herself to look at the man she married. The man she didn't trust. *I can see the pain in his eyes.* How could she do that to him? How could she become someone who didn't trust her husband? Who was suspicious of everyone and everything around her? Didn't she know how hard Ken worked for them to live like this? How compromising he was? *He does it because he loves me.* Who else would ever love her like that? "I'm not used to things being so good for so long. You've seen my family. They're all some level of miserable. I don't know anything else. My brain was looking for a thousand reasons to break up with you."

His grip on her tightened. "You don't want that, right? You don't *want* to break up?"

Lana looked away. "No, baby."

"And I would never do anything to compromise those feelings." Ken cupped his hands around her cheeks, forcing her to look at him again. *How can he look so cool and collected?* She had confessed to thinking he was cheating on her! "You must believe me, Bunny." His thumbs pushed into her flesh, soaking up her tears. "From the moment I met you, all other women paled in comparison. The day you married me was the day I first felt complete."

Most women would cry to hear those words. Most. Lana was not like most women. She often shoved aside those fluttering feelings in order to be practical. To make rational decisions. When Ken asked her to marry him years ago, she didn't say yes right away. She took the time to think it over – for a whole week. For Ken, it was surely torture.

So when she heard him say that, her first reaction wasn't to sob – again – but to fold into his arms and hold him tightly, determined to make him feel *complete* once more.

"We're good, right? You're not worried I'm going to cheat on you, right?"

Lana shook her head. "I ruined your surprise. I was so rude to that girl. I'm fucked up."

"Don't do that to yourself. Although..." Ken gathered her shirt into his fist, pulling against some skin, some hair, and every fiber of her being. "I can't let you get away with this without suffering some consequences, Lana."

He stood, hand lingering around her arm as he gently tugged on it and convinced her to stand up with him. Lana's robe fell from her body, pooling at her feet. *He shouldn't be so transparent.* Except then what would she love on all the time?

"You've been way out of line, Mrs. Andrews." Ken took her by the hips, pushing her against his desk like he had weeks ago. *My husband. My Master.* Lana eased into it, feeling her legs open and her nipples harden beneath her T-shirt. *I need help, all right.* Just five minutes after nearly having her heart broken, she was ready to fuck the man who caught and married her ten years ago. "You're going to have to be dealt with. Between terrorizing the help and daring to doubt my integrity, I'm not even sure where to begin with your punishment."

Lana could hardly look him in the eye.

"Look at this woman I've married." Ken plucked the hem of her shirt and lifted it up, revealing her bare breasts as they responded to the chilly air in her husband's office. "She's already aroused." He pinched one of her nipples; Lana barely responded. "I wish I could say my reasons for marrying you were purely emotional, but I have to admit that your ability to go at any random moment played a huge part. What man wouldn't want a woman ready to go whenever he pleased?"

Lana glanced up at him, her demeanor so demure that her husband looked as if he didn't recognize her – but that look was one only Lana could recognize. To anyone else, Ken looked completely in control of the situation.

"Would you... be pleased to do it right now, Mr. Andrews?"

"Ah, she knows how to make it up to me." Ken stood between her legs, hands rubbing her bare sides as his breathing increased and blood probably rushed to his cock. *He's got me cornered now. Cornered and in need of being published.* For one of the first times ever, though, Lana completely felt it. She knew she needed marital disciplining. She had doubted her husband. She had feared he had turned on her, after so many years of good times and better understanding. How would she have felt were it the other way around? *Horrible. I'd never let him live it down.*

"I want you to feel better after what I've accused you of."

"There are many ways for my wife to make me feel better."

"I'm sure there are, sir." Lana loosened his tie and pulled it off his throat, watching the purple silk slide against his white shirt and curl around her arm. "What should I start with?"

"You? Start? You're misinformed, my love." Ken yanked his tie from her hand and tossed it onto his desk, his figure looming formidably above her, forcing her to sit on the edge of his workspace and search for his lips if she wanted a kiss. And she did. Lana wanted to kiss her husband, to move on, to feel his warmth overtake her and make a renewed woman out of her. "You're going to stand there and be still until I tell you otherwise."

Lana curled her fingers around the edge of the desk, feeling her knuckles tense and turn another color. "Yes, sir." Her thighs were on fire beneath her cotton shorts, even though the room temperature made her shiver without her robe. "Do whatever you want to me, sir."

His thumb trailed down her cheek to her breasts, where her firm nipples made them both react with sexual alacrity. Ken gently kissed his wife's lips, fingers rolling against her nipple and making her freeze in arousal. Lana relaxed her body and prepared to have her husband completely consume her.

"You're still as sexy as you were ten years ago, Bunny," he murmured against her mouth. "Whenever I see you, I want to do nothing more than make endless love to you." He laughed. "Or fuck you senseless. Sometimes there is a difference."

Didn't she know it. They had been exploring that difference for a good twelve years now.

"I don't know how you could think I'm not still madly in love with you after so little time." Ken held fast to her hips, his lips descending the front of her rolled up shirt and pressing against her breasts. Lana gasped as he ran his tongue over her nipple. "Ten years isn't anything, Lana. It would take at least a thousand years to start getting tired of you, and I doubt that would ever happen."

He pulled her shorts down, revealing her smooth skin and finer hair that she kept groomed in part because she liked to, and in part because she always enjoyed the surprise in Ken's eyes when he caught sight of her latest style. Ken forwent that this time, however. He was more preoccupied with nuzzling her slit as he helped her step out of her shorts and lingerie.

"Every time you saunter into this office in your pretty heels, pencil skirts, lingerie, and T-shirts, I have to wonder if you know what kind of effect you still have on me." His finger pushed into her slit, easing her legs open with another moan in her throat. "I know exactly what kind of woman I've married. Even if you come in here to talk dinner or business, I *know* it could very well end with you bent over my desk taking my cock as deep as you can."

Lana shuddered. "I often think that when I come in here."

"Good." Ken tugged on both her nipples, grinning at the amount of whimpers he made her utter. "Because I can't wait to do that to you. Just as soon as you get your first piece of punishment. Do you know what that's going to be?"

They kissed, Lana throwing herself into it as much as Ken did. *I know what it is.* Her hand went to his zipper as her tongue dared his to take over. *I'm not an idiot. I know what this man wants to do to me.* The more she thought about it, the more she fought the urge to drop to her knees right now and beg for forgiveness – the only way she knew how.

"You want me to suck your cock, sir."

"Yes, Bunny. And then I'm going to fuck you."

She didn't think that would be a problem. As she got on her knees and pulled her husband from his pants, all Lana considered was how much this was turning her on.

From enraged that she finally found the evidence that her husband was cheating on her, to this... how else could Lana explain her marriage? *I barely understand it sometimes.* To think that she grew up with the image of men and women being too bored with each other to do this sort of thing. To think she thought her frolic in college would be the most excitement she ever got. *I'd turn in the gangbang and all that if it meant I got to keep Ken for the rest of my life.* Even down there, on her knees, she felt like she did nothing but adore him and the body he offered up whenever the mood struck them.

"That's it." Ken pushed her hair out of the way as she took him into her mouth, stretching her jaw and stretching her small mouth so she could take his hardening shaft and the precum starting to drip from his tip.

Is this better? Am I making it better? Lana didn't know how to shower her husband with affection in any other way. She only knew sexual liberties like sucking him off, playing with other people for his amusement, and feeling him take her every which way imaginable. If someone told her ten years ago that she would not only stay married to Ken for so long, but also have more sex with him than anyone else... *I'd clock you.*

"Good girl." Ken steadied her as he sat in his chair, content to let her do all the work now. Lana knelt between his legs and pleasured him. His tip was thick in her throat, but not as thick as the rest of him filling her mouth and begging to take it in a

A Fragile Wife

few quick strokes. She kept him at bay by wrapping her hand firmly around his base. "You're amazing, Lana."

I'm amazing… Lana pulled off him, looking up into his soft eyes while he twisted her hair around his hand and gave it gentle tugs. "Thank you, sir."

She stroked him, sometimes quickly, sometimes sensually, her body craving his the more she knelt down there and wished he would fuck her. *I'll make you feel amazing…* She sucked his tip, looking at him adoringly, his grunts of approval all Lana needed to feel her body ache, *ache* in ways it hadn't ached for her husband in so long.

"Is this what you want?" She didn't mean to sound so eager, and yet that's how it came out when she took a few moments to speak. "Do you want me on my knees doing this?"

"Yes, baby."

"Are you going to fuck me?"

"No need to sound so innocent, Bunny. I know for a fact that you're anything but."

That's right. Lana was one of the least innocent women she knew. Not always because of Ken… but he was the one who constantly reminded her now. "I'm not, sir." She felt not a drop of shame kneeling there, holding her husband's cock in her hand as she brushed her thumb across the tip. "I'm not innocent at all."

"I wouldn't want you to be innocent. I would much rather have my wife be the dirtiest tramp I've ever met."

Every time he calls me that when we're like this, I get hotter. Lana knew what she was. She knew what she had done in her life and what she wanted to do. She would do it all with Ken – the only man allowed to call her a whore during sex.

"Only for you, sir." With her eyes still locked on his, Lana sucked his tip again, her lips firm against his skin.

"Thing is, Wife, I believe you when you say that. Because I trust you. Now get up. I need to remind you who I spend my time fucking."

Lana pulled herself up. Her shirt fell, covering her breasts and stomach, and with one, stern look from her husband she lifted the white cotton again. *I'm sorry, Husband. Here are my tits. Better now?* Sheesh, she was sometimes too much for her own good.

And so was Ken, who grabbed her, pulled her to him, kissed her throat as if he would suck all the blood from her body, and then shoved her against his desk as she cried in surprise.

"I'm going to fuck you."

As Lana's nipples grazed the top of her husband's desk and her hands braced against the hard wood, Ken pushed the head of his cock into her and made good on his prior promises.

She was maybe half ready. For Lana, that meant a quick, jarring moment of pain and then intense pleasure that nearly took her by storm.

"Oh my God!" she shrieked, the friction shocking her. What shocked her more, however, was how Ken knew to enter her tightness without meeting too much resistance. Only a man who had taken the time over the past decade to learn her body would know how to do that. *"Ken!"*

A Fragile Wife

The miraculous thing – all right, so not miraculous, but damn *crazy* – was how quickly she became wet enough to take more of this. *More!* Lana had a brief moment of concern that sex with her husband would be nothing but discomfort and pain. And then he pulled out long enough to let her get wet... and then it felt like nothing but the greatest thing she could possibly do with the man she married.

"Take it, Lana." His hands gripped her shoulders, keeping her immobile as he roughly thrust into her, forcing her to stretch open and accept every inch of him. Lana held her surprise in, forming a soundless, wordless scream as her mouth contorted into something she would never recognize. As the desk stimulated her nipples, all she could think about was her strong, passionate husband proving to her how he still desired her. "Take me and tell me what you are."

"I'm yours," she whimpered, her entire body shaking. "I'm yours, Mr. Andrews."

He stilled within her. Lana collapsed against the desk, one leg attempting to rise on it if it weren't for Ken pulling it back down.

"You're the only one I need, Wife. Did you hear that? You're my wife." Ken moved again, this time gentler, as if he were making tender love to her. Lana hid her face behind her hand. Everything was almost too much to bear. "That means you're the only one I really need for the rest of my life. Do you believe me?"

It was hard to answer when he was so deep inside her, his cock warm and familiar, yet using her in ways she hadn't felt in so long. "Yes," she whimpered again. "I believe you. You're the only one I really need too."

He pulled out, letting the cold air into her body. *How did he get me that stretched so quickly...* Lana didn't have time to think. Ken yanked her off his desk, hauling her over to the leather sofa he sometimes lounged on. When Lana landed on it, back against leather and left leg swinging over the top of the couch, she knew she wasn't getting off it again until her husband punished and claimed her.

"You're mine, Lana." His growl made her tremble. The buttons popping off his shirt as he quickly disrobed it made her lose herself all over her thighs and the leather beneath her body. "For ten more years, for the rest of my life, I'm not making love to anyone like I make love to you. Now promise me you'll respect my integrity from now on."

"I will!"

"Do you want my cock?" It remained between her spread legs, refusing to enter until she answered. "Tell me you *want* it."

"I do!" Lana didn't just want that. She wanted him, her husband, the man she loved and swore loved her back. "Fuck me, Ken!"

No matter how in charge he was in any situation, Ken could never resist a request like that. He slipped right into her, taking her to his hilt and forcing all his strength into her. Lana cried in ecstasy, in pain, in foreboding as her husband used her as he damn well pleased.

Lana didn't care what others may say about her. She didn't care what she looked like when she had sex. She didn't regard the world as a place where her worth was tied into her role as wife and mistress of a household. In these moments, however, she wanted to believe that the world didn't exist outside of her and Ken anyway. No other man made her feel this way. Now she understood that no other woman made *him* feel this way.

Throwing all that trust back into the man turned her into the person she knew she wanted to be.

"Hell, *Lana.*" Ken grabbed her breasts, driving himself deep within her, searching for the spot that would send her to another realm of reality. *When he does, I'll come, and then he'll come with me.* He once told her that he never orgasmed as hard as he did when he watched her climax. They weren't perfect. There were many times one would finish climaxing before the other began. But when they could be in perfect unison? Lana never felt more in tune with her husband than in those moments. "Fuck me, you're so damned hot."

She was hot? Did the man know what he looked like, with the sweat running down his chest and his slick cock coming in and out of her? Lana grabbed his arms and closed her eyes. "Come in me, Ken," she demanded, stepping out of her bounds. "I want to feel like your wife."

He slipped his hands from her breasts to her neck. "Don't you mean my whore?"

"Same difference."

The way he took her after that was unlike ever before.

There was pain, but it was so satisfying, because it meant she was alive with her husband, here and now. The pain was eclipsed by the intense pleasure rippling through her, attempting to drag Ken down with her into the abyss she carved by herself. *Kill us both and let us rest in peace.* It was morbid to think about death during sex, and yet Lana found it peaceful. They were going to be together for the rest of their lives, carnally and spiritually. One day they would lose the carnally. Was that such a bad thing?

Well, for now she was more than happy to keep the carnal side of things. Especially when she began to climax, her whole body shaking in pleasure and begging to feel her husband come inside her – to reassure her that she was his for now, for eternity.

"Ken!" She dug her fingers into anything they could find: his shoulders, his chest, his hips, the couch… nothing was sacred as the delights of marital bliss overcame her. "I'm coming!"

"I know."

Ken struggled to thrust as intently after that, since Lana's body completely clamped down on him and insisted on keeping him as long as possible. At that point, her husband, her Master, the love of her life had no choice but to give in to his urges.

His hand searched for hers, holding it above her head as the rest of her continued to shake against the couch. Ken made short work of himself, of her, uniting their bodies in the most intimate way he knew how.

No man has ever felt this good inside me. Nor had any man felt as satisfying losing himself inside of her. The deep sounds in his throat… the heat of his body… the arousing scent of their bodies come together. Lana fell into a spell that allowed her to transcend every negative feeling plaguing her heart and mind.

Thank God.

"Holy shit…" Ken collapsed on top of her, still inside her body but unwilling to move. Good. Lana wanted to hold onto this moment a little longer. "I love you, Lana."

She sighed, wrapping her arms around him and nuzzling against his warm form. "I love you too, Kenny."

Their kisses did not lose their intensity for a while. Not when they were so full of the love they reclaimed from one another. *He would never betray me.* Not this man. Not the man who asked her out, who seduced her, who proposed to her, who married her, who spent the past twelve years smitten with her and the fun she brought to their lives. Perhaps with any other woman he would not be so content, but as long as they had each other, there was no reason to believe that anything was other than what it seemed.

When they eventually detached, Lana sitting up while Ken leaned against the back of the couch, she had a new thought. "Do you really think I'm a whore?" she asked. She was prepared for either answer. Ken had heard every sordid story she had to tell a few times over.

"Oh, Bunny, you know that's playing around. I thought you liked it."

"I do. When you're going at me like that, I like it when you call me that." Lana shrugged. "Was just wondering."

"Don't do that." Ken stroked her hair, combing out a few tiny tangles with his fingers. "I want you to take all those negative feelings and forget them. They're not true, Bunny. I love you. I've always loved you. There are no other women… none you're not shoving in my direction, anyway. And if they never came around again? I don't care. I enjoy the fun we have with others, but if it were only you and me for the rest of our days, I'd be as excited to live my life."

She leaned against his shoulder. "I feel the same way."

It felt good to no longer be so paranoid.

Chapter 12

"It's Called Doing Both."

An escape to the Bahamas was what Lana needed after her so far tumultuous winter. Thankfully, a second honeymoon to one of the most exclusive islands in the Caribbean meant lots of warm sunshine and, well, *more*.

It was Day 4, and Lana was already feeling so lazy that she didn't mind spending chunks of change here and there to have waiters bring towels at the pool, drinks at the beach, and sunscreen everywhere in between. The only man allowed to rub it into her skin, however, was her husband Ken. Well, him and the cabana boy tidying up her private oasis by the pool.

"Right there, yes," she purred, watching as the sculpted stud of a young man pressed between her toes. It tickled a little, but Lana was able to ignore it as long as Mr. Hotness kept up his foot rub. *He is so damn fine.* Tanned. Ripped. Just smart enough to know what he was doing but also coasting by on his stunning good looks. The man was a pro at doing whatever Lana told him to do. *He makes a killing seducing married women here.* Hence Mr. Hotness's mini-freakout when Ken approached in his wet swim trunks and a towel wrapped around his shoulders.

"I leave you alone for twenty minutes in this criminally hot black bikini of yours, and lo' and behold, you've got my replacement already."

The cabana boy leaped up, apologized to Mr. Andrews, and took off for the main house a few yards away. This left Ken and Lana alone in their private cabana, although plenty of other resort guests milling about could see what they were up to. *Good.*

"I hate to break it to you, Husband, but the man gave a better foot rub than you could ever hope to do."

"Fascinating. How about some drinks? What do you want, my seductive little vixen?"

With her boy gone, Lana picked up the mock of her husband's memoir, intending to read it... if she didn't get distracted. "I want the biggest, tackiest, most islandy looking drink they have at the bar. Rum, vodka, I don't give a shit. Oh, make it pink."

"One Island Floozy, coming right up."

Ken turned and walked away, taking his firm, muscular ass with him. Lana gazed at it longingly, thinking of how those rock-hard muscles thrust his cock into her the night before as they made love on their balcony. So far every night they had found someplace to do it, whether in their huge bed, the hot tub, the outdoor shower, or right on the beach. *It's been the perfect trip.*

Normally Lana avoided this more public area, but she was a woman with a mission today. Plus, Ken expressed interest in swimming some laps in the Olympic-sized pool. The place was more active than she liked for her vacation, but a couple caught her eye in the neighboring cabana.

She slinked off her lounge chair, leaving behind her husband's book, and sauntered through the shadows until she came upon the stranger couple sitting on a silk-covered bench beneath their awning. The man was perhaps thirty, with strong muscles and a dark outfit that suggested the heat couldn't get to him. Los Angeles. Miami. Maybe Las Vegas. They had to be from one of those hot cities.

The woman, on the other hand, was thin, with short, bobbed brown hair and modest breasts packed into a blue bikini top. The way she stroked her male companion's arm – giving Lana a great view of the diamond wedding ring on the woman's left hand – suggested a long familiarity. *Bingo.*

"Come here often?" she asked, leaning against a pillar. "To this island, I mean."

As it turned out, it was their first time visiting. They were on their yearly vacation after being married a whole five years. When Lana mentioned her husband of ten years was around there somewhere, they both expressed amazement that she was old enough to be married for ten years. *Stop. You flatter me.*

Cynthia Dane

"I see my flirty wife has invaded the neighbors' cabana," Ken said, bringing his wife a fizzy pink drink with a lemon-colored straw. "She's not bothering you, is she?"

As laughter took the four of them over, Lana kissed her husband's cheek before redirecting her lips to his ear.

"Code red, Kenny."

He slipped his arm around her midsection. "I figured. She's totally your type."

"And he's totally yours."

"I thought we weren't doing this on our honeymoon."

"I changed my mind. I wanna make him watch you fuck his wife while I give him the hummer of his life."

"That's boring. I was thinking one giant pile in our cottage."

"It's called doing both."

Lana patted her husband's shoulder and went back to the main conversation at hand. "Of course we've been to Vermont," she said. "Kenneth has family from there."

Idle chitchat always had a habit of leading to something more… risqué. Which proved true even now as Mr. and Mrs. Andrews flattered their new friends into submission. Quite literally.

I don't want to have any other kind of marriage. Lana walked back to her cottage with her husband and friends, arms linking between Ken's and the woman's. She looked at her husband, sharing with him a small smile that said he infinitely loved her. *I've got everything I could possibly need in this one right here.*

A Fragile Wife

She wasn't fragile – she was cautious. Cautious to the strange sensations that sometimes struck her heart and soul. The two parts of her most susceptible to wild speculation and suggestion.

Ten years had gone by so quickly. She hoped the next ten with her husband would be a bit more relaxed. Anywhere outside of the bedroom, anyway.

Cynthia Dane

A Fragile Wife

Cynthia Dane spends most of her time writing in the great Pacific Northwest. And when she's not writing, she's dreaming up her next big plot and meeting all sorts of new characters in her head.

She loves stories that are sexy, fun, and cut right to the chase. You can always count on explosive romances - both in and out of the bedroom - when you read a Cynthia Dane story.

Falling in love. Making love. Love in all shades and shapes and sizes. Cynthia loves it all!

Connect with Cynthia on any of the following:

Website: http://www.cynthiadane.com
Twitter: http://twitter.com/cynthia_dane
Facebook: http://facebook.com/authorcynthiadane

Printed in Great Britain
by Amazon

40690095R00118